Prologue

The white men came to the Green River country early in the Grass Moon. Seven big men on seven big horses, leading a pack string of ten more. They made camp that first night in a verdant meadow along a tributary of the Green known as Ham's Fork to the whites and Dead Elk Creek to the Shoshones.

The whites made no secret of their coming. They were loud and boisterous. They joked and laughed a lot, but the warriors who watched from concealment noticed that the laughter did not touch their eyes. As was typical of whites, they built their campfire twice as large as it should be, a fire so bright it could be seen from far off.

Word was brought to the leader of the Green River Shoshones. Touch the Clouds was a giant in stature as well as reputation, a warrior universally respected by his people. Not since the days of Moh-Woom-Ho had one of their number been so highly regarded. In important matters he was

1

always consulted. In councils his views always held the most weight. So when he advised his people to let the whites go their way in peace, the Shoshones were content to go on about their own lives. As a precaution, though, Touch the Clouds did send a pair of warriors back to continue watching the intruders until the whites had passed through Shoshone territory.

Then a strange thing happened.

The whites did not move on. They stayed another sleep, and yet a third, and by the fourth day they were busy chopping trees and dragging them to the center of the meadow, where the whites trimmed and notched them.

The two young warriors sent to spy on the whites did not know what to make of it. They soon realized the whites were constructing a wooden lodge of considerable size, but what it might portend, they were at a loss to guess. The youngest, Runs Across the River, raced to their village to relay the news.

A council was called. Touch the Clouds had the seat of honor. On his right was Drags the Rope, another venerable warrior. On his left was Wis-Kin, or Cut Hair, whose wrinkled face testified to his years and his wisdom. The lodge was jammed. The Shoshones attached great importance to their dealings with whites, and took great pride in the fact that of all the tribes in the central Rockies, they alone had never lifted a white scalp. The Crows, the Utes, the Blackfeet, the Dakotas, all had taken white lives. But not the Shoshones. Their leaders advocated peace.

Touch the Clouds listened with great interest to the young warrior's account. When Runs Across the River was done, murmuring broke out.

As usual, Hungry Wolf was first to voice his opinion. And, as usual, his sentiments were laced with suspicion and hostility. "Once again the whites treat our land as if it is theirs," he declared. "I have seen these wooden lodges before. The white called Brid-ger, the one we call Blanket

Chief, has built a great wooden lodge many sleeps to the south. It is as tall as the trees and has room inside for a hundred. This new one will be the same. More whites will come. They will hunt our forests and fish our streams. Our women and children will go hungry that the whites may feed their bellies." He paused for effect. "I say we go to these whites. We tell them this land is our land and they must build their lodge elsewhere."

All eyes swung toward Touch the Clouds. "I, too, have visited the Blanket Chief's lodge," he slowly began, choosing his words with care. "His family and two other whites live there with him. That is all. And they do not kill more game than they need." He swept those assembled with his piercing gaze. "How can we say these new whites will do any different when we do not know them or why they have come?"

"So you propose we do nothing?" Hungry Wolf challenged. "I say that if we let these new whites build their lodge in the middle of our territory, before too many winters we will have whites everywhere we look. We must drive them out, now, before their numbers increase."

Some of the younger warriors voiced their agreement. The young were always more ready to go to war than those who had experienced it.

Touch the Clouds squared his broad shoulders and placed his brawny hands on his knees. "That is Ute talk. Or Blackfoot talk. They regard the whites as enemies. Since when do we do the same? Have the whites ever wronged us? No. Have they ever attacked us? No. They have offered us the hand of friendship and we have accepted. We have even adopted one of their own into our tribe." He was referring to Nate King, better known as Grizzly Killer. King's wife, Wi-no-na, was Touch the Clouds's cousin.

Hungry Wolf went to respond, but Drags the Rope spoke first, saying, "What do you suggest we do, Touch the Clouds?"

3

"We watch these whites. We see what they are about. And when the time is right, I will pay them a visit."

Hungry Wolf and the antiwhite faction did not like the decision, but they were not about to oppose Touch the Clouds openly.

Over the course of the next moon, the white men erected not one but four lodges. The largest was twenty paces wide and forty paces long, and over the entrance they hung a short plank bearing painted symbols. The second lodge was half that size, and was where the white men slept at night. The third lodge was the smallest and most peculiar. Before building it, the whites dug a deep hole. Then, to the amazement of the warriors secreted in the undergrowth, they constructed the lodge right on top of it. For all that effort, the whites went into the small lodge only a couple of times a day and never stayed very long. A rank odor was undoubtedly to blame. Along about the fourth day after it was completed, every time the door opened, the Shoshones smelled the most awful stink.

The last lodge the whites built was for their horses. The whites always barred it at night. In the daytime the horses were not permitted to run free, but were instead penned in a corral adjacent to the horse lodge. The whites spent several days cutting grass and hauling it inside, piling a stack higher than a man's head.

The Shoshones knew why the whites didn't let their animals graze freely. The whites were afraid they would be stolen. What with regular Blackfoot and Crow forays into Shoshone country, their fear was justified.

It was to the whites' credit that they never strayed far from the meadow unless they went in pairs. And every white man always had his guns with him—a long rifle and a brace of pistols. They were always vigilant, always alert.

The Shoshones suspected the whites knew they were being spied on. But either the whites knew the Shoshones were friendly, or the whites were uncommonly brave, for they showed no fear and took no extra precautions.

Then came the morning, one moon after the whites arrived, that one of their number walked alone across the meadow to the bank of Dead Elk Creek. The Shoshones had taken to calling him Crooked Nose, because his nose had once been broken and never healed properly. Crooked Nose carried a new rifle, an ammunition pouch, and a stick. When he reached the bank, he jammed the stick into the ground, propped the rifle against it, and draped the ammo pouch over both. Stepping back, he turned toward the woods where the spies were hidden, motioned as if beckoning, and jabbered at some length in the white tongue.

Warriors from Touch the Clouds's village had been taking turns keeping watch. The two there at the time, Bear's Backbone and Sitting Eagle, glanced at each other, unsure what to do. They saw the white man turn and go into the long lodge. None of the others were out and about.

"Why did he leave the gun there?" Sitting Eagle wondered.

"It is a stupid thing to do," Bear's Backbone said. "A Crow or a Blackfoot could come and steal it."

"Or one of us could run out there and grab it," Sitting Eagle proposed.

"What if it is a ruse?" Bear's Backbone countered. "What if they are trying to lure us out into the open so they can shoot us?" Bear's Backbone began to back away from the thicket screening them. "Touch the Clouds must hear of this. He will know what to do. He is more familiar with white ways."

By noon Bear's Backbone reached the village. A council was called, and it was decided to send a formal delegation to visit the whites and ascertain their motives. Touch the Clouds led the party of twenty-six warriors. They arrived at Dead Horse Creek by nightfall but stayed well off in the trees.

"We will wait for morning to talk to them," Touch the

Clouds said. In order to demonstrate their peaceful intentions, he had a fire kindled where the whites were bound to notice it. He and the other warriors sat around the fire until late, talking and generally making more noise than they ordinarily would.

Dawn broke, and Touch the Clouds and his close friend of many years, Drags the Rope, led ten Shoshones on foot toward the wooden lodges. As Touch the Clouds anticipated, the whites were expecting a visit, and when he was a stone's throw from the door, it opened and out filed the seven whites. He was encouraged to see that none were armed.

The white man with the crooked nose stepped out in front and smiled broadly, displaying a mouth full of teeth yellowed by tobacco stains and neglect. "We welcome our red brothers," he said in his own tongue.

Drags the Rope translated. Thanks to his close acquaintance with a white trapper when he was very young, and later with Nate King, he spoke more than adequate English. Only Nate's wife spoke the white tongue more fluently.

The leader's greeting mildly surprised Touch the Clouds. While most whites were friendly enough to his people, he was aware that many white men disliked and distrusted the "red man." Some went so far as to believe that the only good Indian was a dead one. "Tell him that if he speaks with a straight tongue, we welcome them."

The white man's smile widened after Drags the Rope conveyed the tidings. He had round cheeks and a round belly, and his clothes were unkempt. Stubble sprinkled his double chin, and his hair looked greasy. "My name is Borke. Artemis Borke." He looked Touch the Clouds up and down and softly whistled. "You sure are a big 'un. I reckon you're the buck we've heard so much about. The chief of the Green River Snakes."

"I am Touch the Clouds."

Borke glanced at one of the others, who smirked and nodded. "We could tell by your buckskins and hair that you were friendlies. Truth is, we've been hopin' you would pay us a visit. We have a business proposition to talk over. But first," Borke nodded toward the creek bank where the rifle was still propped, "have one of your bucks fetch that long gun."

Drags the Rope relayed the request. Shoulder Blade promptly moved toward Dead Elk Creek.

"We put it out as a gift for you," Borke explained. "As a token of the value we place in earning your favor."

"Why are you here?" Touch the Clouds inquired through his friend.

Borke snickered. "You're not one for beatin' around the bush, are you, Chief? Fair enough. My pards and I aim to open a tradin' post. If your people bring us things we're interested in, we'll see to it they get all the guns, blankets, and foofaraw they want."

Touch the Clouds studied the other whites. They were sculpted from the same clay as Artemis Borke—rough-hewn, unshaven, hard. All wore smiles. Yet Touch the Clouds felt a vague sense of unease.

"We would like to have your permission, chief," Borke had gone on. "We know this is Snake country. We know it wouldn't be right to conduct business without your say-so. So how about it?"

"A trading post?" Touch the Clouds had been to Bent's Fort a few times, and once to Fort Hall. To reach either involved a ride of many days. The idea of having a trading post in the heart of Shoshone territory appealed to him, but he did not want the whites to think he was too eager.

"You heard correctly, hoss," Borke said, nodding. "All the goods your people will ever want, right here for the askin'. Blankets for your squaws. Hard candy for your sprouts. Guns for every warrior."

At that juncture Shoulder Blade walked up with the new rifle and ammo pouch and gave them to Touch the Clouds.

David Thompson

The rifle was a Hawken, favored by Nate King and frontiersmen everywhere, not an inferior trade rifle like those foisted on Indians by the Hudson's Bay Company. Touch the Clouds ran his huge hand over the smooth metal.

"Like it, do you?" Borke asked, chuckling. "Who wouldn't? And it's yours, Chief. With our blessin'."

"Mine?" Touch the Clouds said when Drags the Rope relayed the news. He had never owned a white man's weapon before. His ash bow and long lance had always served him in good stead. But from time to time he had entertained the thought of trying a gun for a while to see if they were as reliable and deadly as some claimed.

"Haven't you been listenin' to a word I've told you? Yes, yours, free of charge. To prove we speak with straight tongues."

Several other warriors, Touch the Clouds observed, were eyeing the rifle with obvious envy.

"Give it a try," Borke prompted. "If you need help loadin' it, we'll be glad to show you how." Brazenly, he came forward and placed a grimy hand on Touch the Clouds's forearm. "Think what it would mean if all your braves had guns like this! Think how powerful it will make your people." He lowered his voice conspiratorially. "We know about the problems the Snakes have been havin' with the Crows, the Dakotas, the Blackfeet, and the Utes. They raid your villages. They steal your horses. But not anymore! Not if all your bucks are armed with the latest and best rifles on the market."

Drags the Rope was translating loudly enough for the rest of the warriors to hear, and excited whispering erupted.

"We're not askin' you to decide right this moment," Borke said. "Go back to your people. Palaver a spell. See what they want. Then get back to us with your decision. We won't start up our post without your consent."

Touch the Clouds idly wondered why, if that was the case, the whites had already built it. He had to admit he

8

was growing as excited as his friends, but he had the welfare of his people to think of and must not let his personal feelings sway his decision. "Tell me. Do you know Nate King?"

The question caused Artemis Borke to blink. "Sure I do, hoss. Who hasn't heard of him? He's been livin' in these mountains goin' on twenty years now. Has him a Shoshone squaw, too."

Touch the Clouds looked the trader in the eyes. "Tell this man, Drags the Rope, that we do not like it when our women are called 'squaws.' " Nate King had informed him the term was derogatory, a slur on the virtue of their wives and daughters.

Borke laughed good-naturedly. "My apologies, Chief. Old habits are hard to break. You'll never hear any of us call one of your women a squaw again." He clapped Touch the Clouds on the shoulder. "As for Nate King, I've run into him now and again. Folks say he's as honorable as the year is long." Borke's bushy eyebrows pinched together. "Why'd you ask, anyhow?"

"He is one of us."

"A Snake? I thought he was—" Catching himself, Borke chuckled. "Oh. I recollect now. Your tribe adopted him, is that it? Well, you couldn't have made a better choice if you tried."

Touch the Clouds considered Nate King a virtual brother. To hear this praise pleased him immensely. "We will hold a council," he declared. "In three sleeps I will return with our decision." Wheeling, he reentered the forest, Drags the Rope and the rest at his heels.

Artemis Borke grinned and waved as the Shoshones melted into the vegetation. When they were out of earshot, he winked at his companions and gleefully rubbed his hands together. "What did I tell you, boys? Dumber than stumps, the whole kit and caboodle. Before you know it, we'll have 'em eatin' out of our hands."

Chapter One

The tracks were plain as day.

Sometime in the middle of the night a bear had wandered out of the woods to the south, made a circuit of the clearing, then ambled close to their cabin and corral, and to their horses.

It had been months since a bear wandered into their remote valley, and Nate King had to determine whether the roving bruin posed a threat to his family and their livestock. Examining the prints, he was encouraged to discover it was a black bear, not a grizzly. Judging from the size and the scat, he judged it to be a young male.

The tracks led to a trail that linked their cabin to a large lake. Hefting his rifle, Nate jogged through a tract of towering pines and on down to the water's edge. There the bear had stopped to slake its thirst, then roved northward along the shore.

Nate wasn't worried about running into it. In addition to

his Hawken, he had a pair of large-caliber smoothbore flint-lock pistols wedged under his wide leather belt on either side of his buckle. He also had a Bowie knife on his left hip, a tomahawk on the right. Buckskins clung to his powerful frame, and knee-high moccasins adorned his feet. Completing his personal portrait were emerald-green eyes and raven-black hair.

About to continue on, Nate heard the patter of small feet to his rear and pivoted. A pint-sized bundle of energy wearing a green homespun dress and black shoes skipped toward him.

"Pa! Why didn't you wait for me?" his twelve-year-old daughter, Evelyn, demanded.

"Your mother said she had chores for you to do," Nate responded. "I figured it would be a while before you were free."

"I talked Ma into letting me come along." Evelyn grinned. Like him, she had striking green eyes and coal-black hair, but her oval face and lovely features were inherited from her Shoshone mother. "Doing the dishes and washing clothes can wait."

Every morning Nate made a sweep of their homestead looking for sign of hostiles or dangerous beasts. Every morning Evelyn tagged along. It was ritual with them—just as it had been with Nate and her older brother, Zach, who now had a wife of his own and a homestead of his own several valleys over.

"Have you found something?" Evelyn asked.

"Tracks," Nate disclosed, pointing.

Evelyn examined the impressions. "A black bear, I take it. Three, maybe four winters old. Nothing for us to fret about, right?"

"Right," Nate confirmed, proud at her display of wood-craft. She had learned the lessons he'd taught her well, and despite her tender years could hold her own with most mountaineers. Too bad, he reflected, his instruction was all for naught. For some time now she had been expressing a desire to move to the States when she was old enough.

"Do we follow it anyhow to see where it got to?"

"That we do." The morning was brisk and bright and a variety of birds were gaily chirping. Nate breathed deep, and smiled. It was grand to be alive. Doubly so, since when his oldest flew the coop, he had learned to appreciate how precious every moment spent with his children truly was.

Evelyn wagged her .31-caliber custom-made rifle in the direction the bear had gone. "Likely he's over the mountains by now."

"Let's hope so," Nate agreed. He refused to abide potential threats to his family, four-legged or otherwise. Consequently, he made it a point to drive off every bear, painter, and wolverine tempted to stake out the valley as its own.

Resting her rifle across her shoulder, Evelyn marched briskly at his side, taking two steps for each of his. "Ma did say we could use a new bearskin rug. The one in front of the fireplace is worn to a frazzle."

Their current rug had made the mistake of trying to break into their corral to get at their horses, forcing Nate to drop it with a shot to the brainpan. That had been seven years ago, and the rug had sustained a lot of wear and tear in the interim. But the truth be told, Nate wasn't particularly eager to kill the one they were trailing. It hadn't done them any harm.

"Mind if I ask you a question, Pa?"

"Ask away, daughter," Nate said. Of late she had turned into a fount of queries, most dealing with life in the white man's world. This time was no exception.

"You grew up in New York City. You've been to New Orleans and Santa Fe and such." Evelyn looked up. "What's it like living in places like that?"

Nate patted her head. "You've asked that question fifty times if you've asked it once. I should think you would have my answer memorized by now."

"Tell me again. Please."

Sighing, Nate cradled his Hawken in the crook of an elbow. "It's nothing like life here. There are more people than you can shake a stick at, for one thing. The streets are jammed every hour of the day and most of the night, and you need to be mighty careful crossing them or you're liable to be run down—"

"What about the ladies?"

In his mind's eye, Nate flashed back to his younger years and some of the girls he had known before he headed for the frontier. "They wear the prettiest dresses they can afford and spend a lot of their free time shopping for new ones. They have a passion for the theater, and will go every chance they get. They're also fond of balls and socials, and will spend half the night dancing if given the chance. They like to have their hair done up real fancy-like. And to paint their nails." He summed up his assessment with, "Mostly, they just like to have fun."

"I want to live like they do!" Evelyn exclaimed. "To wear fine clothes everywhere! To eat at restaurants! To take a carriage wherever I need to go!" Clasping her hands to her bosom, Evelyn sighed happily. "It will be heavenly."

Nate would rather she preferred mountain life to city living, but she had her mind made up. "All you think about are the good aspects. You never give any thought to the bad."

"To so many people a person can't hardly breathe without bumping into someone else? To the soot in the air in the winter? To the smell of horse droppings all the time? To the footpads who will steal me blind as soon as look at me?" Evelyn bobbed her oval chin. "I never forget a word you say."

"Yet you still intend on leaving us," Nate said sadly.

"I'm sorry, Pa. I know it upset Ma and you something terrible. But I want to go. Maybe I won't like it. Maybe city life isn't as grand as I think it is. But the only way I'll find out is if I live in one for a spell."

"That's true," Nate conceded. "But I think you'll find that living here has a lot to recommend it, too."

"Maybe so. But in the States, folks can go outside without having to worry about being eaten by a grizzly. Or jumped by a mountain lion. Or bitten by a rattlesnake. Or having their scalp lifted by hostiles." Evelyn sighed. "Want me to go on?"

"Is that the real reason you want to leave? All the dangers here?" Nate couldn't blame her if it was. In the wild the cost of self-preservation was eternal vigilance. It didn't do to let one's guard down for an instant. And he would be the first to admit it became mighty tiresome after a while. Always being alert, always living on edge, chafed at the nerves and ate at the soul. Some couldn't take the strain.

"Why put up with stuff like that when we don't have to?"

Once again, Nate was impressed by his offspring's insight. She was wise beyond her tender years, a trait he attributed to her mother's influence. "Your ma and I have talked it over. Whatever you decide is fine by us. If you want to go to the States, we'll take you there and help set you up on your own. But don't hold it against us if we don't jump up and down with joy."

Evelyn giggled. "You make it sound as if you'll never see me again once I'm gone. I promise I'll come visit you as often as can be. And heck, it's years yet before I'm leaving. So why be so upset?"

Thankfully for Nate, the bear's tracks veered into the pines, giving him an excuse to nip their talk in the bud and concentrate on something else. Guided by its nose, the bear had wound through the heavy woodland to a log, which it had ripped to bits seeking grubs. From there, the hairy intruder had meandered toward a high ridge that separated their sanctuary from the outside world.

"It's not heading for one of the passes," Evelyn observed.

No, it wasn't, Nate mused. And that meant it had bedded down somewhere in their valley instead of leaving. "I'll take you on home and go out after him on my own."

Evelyn halted and folded her arms across her chest. "Why can't we do it together? I won't get in your way."

"You're the one who doesn't like danger, remember?" Nate wasn't trying to rub her nose in it. Her welfare was his utmost concern.

"What danger? It's a black bear. They hardly ever attack people."

"Hardly ever," Nate stressed. There were exceptions. He recalled a Flathead who had been off elk hunting with friends. At one point the warrior followed fresh elk tracks into a thicket, and the next thing his companions knew, out of it burst the most horrendous screams and roars. A sleeping black bear hadn't taken kindly to almost being stepped on. The warrior was laid up in his lodge for months and his face was forever disfigured.

Another time, several young Shoshone women were off picking berries when out of the berry patch appeared a black bear. The women yelled to shoo it off, but the bear had other ideas. It knocked one of the women down, tearing her leg open from knee to hip, then bit down on her shoulder and proceeded to drag her off. The screams of her friends brought warriors on the run. Four arrows ended the bear's life, while the young woman spent the rest of hers a cripple.

"I'm not worried when I'm with you," Evelyn was saying. "They don't call you Grizzly Killer for nothing."

As one of the first whites to settle in the Rockies, it had been Nate's misfortune to tangle with grizzlies on more occasions than he cared to count. Back then, the monsters had been everywhere. Trappers and mountain men had thinned their ranks considerably, and although Nate still ran into one on occasion, he hadn't had to kill a griz in a coon's age.

Again the tracks veered, this time to the northeast, and

soon emerged from the forest fifty yards from the ridge. Littered with boulders and crisscrossed by dry washes and ravines, it was an ideal resting spot for a tired bear.

"It'll be awful hard flushing him out of there, won't it?" Evelyn asked.

That it would. "I want you to stay here and wait for me," Nate said, adding quickly when she opened her mouth, "And not a lick of protest, or I'll find even more chores for you to do."

"Ahh, Pa," Evelyn pouted. "I'm a big girl now. I can take care of myself."

"You heard me."

The prints guided Nate to the mouth of a steep-sided coulee. Pressing the Hawken's stock to his shoulder, he warily entered it. The walls blotted out the sun, plunging him in shadow. He didn't like being hemmed in, didn't like not having much room to maneuver if the bear came at him.

A bend was ahead. Nate approached it slowly, placing each foot down with care. A peek revealed another straight stretch. It also showed him that the walls narrowed to a width of five to six feet. A scowl creased Nate's countenance. For all he knew, the coulee might end farther in. The last thing he wanted was to accidentally trap the black bear back in there with no other way out. No animal liked to be cornered.

Beads of sweat broke out on Nate's brow. Attributing it to the heat of the day, he moved on. He was conscious of the lack of wind, of oppressive silence, of the faint, inadvertent scrape of his moccasin. A second bend appeared. He was six feet from it when an ominous growl filled the coulee.

Nate stopped dead. The bear had either caught his scent or heard him. Sidling to the right, he tried to catch a glimpse of it but couldn't. Another growl, louder and more guttural, warned him it was growing agitated. He had to do something or it might attack. Thinking to scare it out the other

end of the coulee—provided the coulee *had* another end—
he shouted, "Ho! Bear! Light a shuck before I blow out your
wick!"

Taut silence fell. Nate strained his ears but couldn't hear
a thing. Still hoping to drive it away rather than kill it, he
stomped his foot and hollered, "Get out of here, damn you!
Go make a nuisance of yourself somewhere else!"

Nate inwardly chuckled at his own foolishness. Here he
was, going to all this effort to spare the animal's life, when
most mountaineers would shoot it down without a second
thought. "What's it going to be?" he yelled.

Again, a deep silence. Nate inched forward, his thumb
on the Hawken's hammer, his forefinger curled around the
trigger. He couldn't hear heavy breathing, which he con-
strued as a good sign. Maybe the bear was already gone.

"Pa?"

Evelyn's faint cry was muted by the high walls. Without
thinking, Nate turned his head to answer. At that very instant, a roar shook the coulee and the black bear hurtled
around the bend, charging straight at him. Nate barely had
time to pivot before the bear slammed into him like a living
battering ram.

Too late, Nate squeezed the trigger. The ball tore into the
ground, not the bear, as Nate was upended like a sliver of
straw in a gale. He tumbled head over heels and hit the left-
hand wall with jarring impact.

Another roar reverberated.

Nate struggled to his knees and saw the bear coming at
him with its long fangs bared. He had lost the Hawken, but
he still had his .55-caliber pistols, either of which could
down the beast at short range. Whipping them out, he extended them and thumbed back the hammers to shoot.

The bear never gave him the chance. In a black blur it
was on top of him, its claw-tipped paws flashing.

A powerful blow flung Nate back against the wall. His
left pistol went flying. Dazed, he brought the right one up

and was seared by intense pain in his shoulder. The bear's jaws were clamped fast. He could feel its teeth grate on bone. Their eyes met, mere inches apart, and the sight of those blazing dark orbs glaring balefully into his galvanized Nate into shoving the pistol's muzzle against the bear's neck and stroking the trigger.

It didn't have the desired effect.

Rumbling deep in its barrel chest, the black bear reared back, hauling Nate along with it. A bruising paw struck Nate's arm, another clipped him on the side of the head. He was shaken much as a terrier would shake a squirrel, then suddenly slung flat onto his back. Blinking, he saw the bear straddle him, saw its maw gape wide, and felt sticky saliva drip onto his neck and face.

"Let my pa be!"

It took several seconds for the defiant cry to register. Nate and the black bear both twisted their necks. There, not ten feet away, stood Evelyn. She had her rifle elevated and was taking a bead on the bear's head.

"Evelyn, run!" Nate bawled. Her Hawken was meant for small game. It lacked the kick to drop a bear and would only enrage it further. "Get out of here!" If she didn't, the beast might rip her to ribbons. "Fetch your mother!"

His shouts brought the renewed wrath of the bear down on his head. Nate winced as claws raked his forehead. Warm blood spurted, covering his right eye and threatening to blind his left, as well. He tried to roll aside, but the bear smashed a paw onto his chest, pinning him.

"I told you to let him be!" Evelyn cried. Her rifle cracked.

The bear snarled and swiveled.

Fearing for her life, Nate did the only thing he could. He flung his left arm around the bear's neck and clung on fast while simultaneously drawing his Bowie and burying it to the hilt just under the bear's protruding jaw. More blood flowed. But whether it was his or the bear's, Nate couldn't say. A paw nearly tore him loose as he was dragged toward

Evelyn. Frantic, he sank the blade in again and again and again.

Evelyn shouted something he couldn't quite hear. The bear was almost on top of her. Nate wrenched with all his strength, and the animal staggered. There was another roar, the loudest yet, and they both crashed to the ground, Nate buried under hundreds of pounds of solid brawn. He kept on stabbing, stabbing, stabbing. His vision blurred, the world a red haze, but he didn't stop.

"Pa! Enough! He's done for!"

Small hands gripped Nate's wrist and wouldn't let go. He let his arm go limp and rubbed his face against the bear's hide to wipe the blood off his eyes. Evelyn swam into focus. "Are you all right?" Her own eyes were brimming with tears. "Did it hurt you?"

"I'm fine," Evelyn said, her face chalk-white. "But Pa, you . . ." She couldn't bring herself to finish what she was going to say.

Nate glanced down and felt something flap against his eyes. Reaching up, he discovered it was a flap of his own skin, peeled from his forehead like an apple skin from an apple. His shoulders, chest, and legs were a maze of slashes and cuts, and he was bleeding profusely. Weakness assailed him and bile rose in his throat. Choking it down, he girded himself to stand and placed both hands flat under him.

"Don't, Pa! You'd never make it home, the shape you're in. Lie real still while I run and fetch Ma."

"I can manage," Nate insisted. But when he started to stand, the weakness worsened and a tidal wave of dizziness washed over him. He sank back, a loud groan escaping his lips.

"Hang on," Evelyn said encouragingly while backing down the coulee. "I won't be long."

"All I need is a minute or two to rest up," Nate said. But she wasn't there to hear. Turning his neck, he caught sight of her rounding the far bend. Her worry, her love, brought a knot to his throat. She was a good girl, that child of his, and would do any parent proud.

About to close his eyes, Nate was startled by a noise from close at hand. Thinking the bear wasn't done for, he clutched at his tomahawk. But the brute was as limp as a wet rag and leaking blood like a sieve; its sides weren't moving, its lips were slack. It was as dead as dead could be. So what made the noise?

Using his left hand for leverage, Nate propped himself against the wall. The ground was damp and sticky, his buckskins drenched scarlet. Palely gleaming bone was visible through the gash in his shoulder.

The irony didn't escape him. After all the grizzlies Nate had slain, to be nearly done in by a puny black bear was downright humiliating.

Nate grinned at the notion. Ever so slowly, he sat up. His shoulder and a wound in his thigh were bleeding the worst. He had to stop the flow, but he had nothing to stop it with. Or did he? He could cut his shirt into strips to use as tourniquets. His Bowie, though, was still embedded in the bear. His tomahawk, which he kept honed to a sharp edge, might suffice.

Weariness oozing from every pore, Nate tried to slip his shirt off over his head. He was asking the impossible. To hell with it, then, he thought, and slumped back. He was so ungodly tired, he didn't feel like lifting a finger. Shutting his eyes, he grit his teeth against ripples of pain and hoped he could stay conscious until his wife got there. Winona would take good care of him. A wizard with herbs and roots, she knew of medicinal concoctions white doctors had never heard of. Tremendously effective ointments and the like.

Again Nate heard a noise. Cracking his eyelids, he scanned the coulee but saw nothing to account for it. The bear was where it had fallen. And it would be half an hour or so before Winona showed up.

His drowsiness growing, Nate let his mind drift. He recollected his initial trek to the Rockies in the company of his favorite uncle, and how events conspired to strand him in the wilderness. Most people would regard it as a calamity, yet out of it came great happiness. For eventually he met Winona, and now had a family and home he held preciously dear.

In the scheme of things, Nate counted himself supremely lucky. He had a wife who loved him, heart and soul. He had two children who had grown as straight as ramrods. He lived in the mountains he cherished, surrounded by majestic peaks and pristine natural beauty. And he was free, truly free, with no one trying to tell him what he should and shouldn't do. No one trying to lord it over him.

Nate hadn't truly appreciated true freedom until he left civilization and the invisible bars of his cage were gone. Before he came west, he had been at the beck and call of a tyrannical boss who treated him with ill-concealed contempt and worked him long hours for scant pay, all the while acting as if it were the biggest favor anyone ever did him.

Civilization was peculiar in that regard. The rich lived in vaults of luxury while the poor struggled for scraps for their next meal. Politicians claimed they always had everyone's best interests at heart while secretly lining their pockets with all the money they could hoard. Laws were enforced differently for those with bulging wallets and those without.

Nate wanted none of that. He had always had a strong dislike of hypocrisy, and the life he had forsaken reeked of it. Folks always putting on airs, always pretending to be something other than what they were. Give him the honest, unfettered life of a frontiersman any day.

Against his will, Nate dozed off. He slept fitfully, his rest broken by snatches of chaotic dreams.

Then a rattling sound snapped Nate fully awake. Small stones and dirt were cascading down the opposite wall. He looked up and saw a shadow flit across the top of the coulee. His pulse quickened, and he placed his hand on his tomahawk.

Somewhere beyond the coulee a bird squawked. To the south, mere specks in the firmament, several buzzards circled.

More stones clattered, originating from a cluster of boulders on the rim. Nate scoured them with care but saw nothing to be alarmed about. Then there was a flicker of movement and he spotted a tawny snake jerking from side to side.

A snake, Nate knew, attached to a feline form crouched behind the boulders. *Attached to a mountain lion.* His rifle was out of reach. He might be able to crawl to a pistol, but could he load it? He doubted he had the energy.

The cat's tail stiffened, and the next instant the painter raised its head. Cold, slanted eyes fixed on the bear, switched to Nate, and swung back again. Nate figured the big cat had heard the ruckus and slunk close to investigate. Now the aroma of spilled blood had enticed it into the open and put it in a mind to help itself to a meal.

Nate pried at his tomahawk, trying to slide it out from under his belt. His fingers felt thick and awkward, and his arms were as sluggish as snails. If the cat pounced, he wouldn't be able to lift a finger to defend himself.

As if the predator had read his thoughts, it rose higher and stepped from behind the boulders. Brilliant sunlight bathed a magnificent male of the species. Sinews rippling under its sleek hide, it moved to the edge and crouched to leap.

Nate opened his mouth to shout, but his mouth and throat were too dry. All that came out was a pitiable croak. Licking his lips, he swallowed a few times and squawked, "Get out of here, you mangy painter!"

The sound of a human voice ordinarily gave wild creatures pause. Some mountaineers believed the Good Lord instilled a fear of man in all wildlife. They saw mankind as the masters of creation and the beasts as naturally subservient. All a man had to do was show he had no fear and an animal would go running off with its tail tucked between its legs.

That was their notion, anyway. Nate had indeed scared off many a cougar and many a bear with loud shouts, but it didn't always work. And it didn't work now. Instead of backing off, the big cat snarled and hissed and dug its claws into the earth.

"This just isn't my day," Nate said softly.

The next moment, the mountain lion leaped.

Chapter Two

The day had started as most any other.

Situated on a grassy belt adjacent to the Green River, the Shoshone encampment was arranged in traditional fashion. The hundred-plus lodges, many decorated with symbols, were arranged in large circles, their openings to the east. Nearby were hundreds of horses, grazing under the watchful eyes of young boys. Young girls were accompanying their mothers to the river for water.

Touch the Clouds gazed across the camp and smiled in serene satisfaction. He had just pushed the flap to his lodge aside and unfurled to his full height to greet the new dawn, as was his custom. A sparkling blue sheen marked the winding course of the river. Beyond it grew dense forest, the tops of the trees framed by a rosy glow. Stretching out his long arms, he sang a chant of praise to Dam Apua.

Mornings were Touch the Clouds's favorite time of day. The world and all in it were so fresh, so new. He thanked the Father for his being alive, for his three wives and seven children, and asked for continued guidance in leading his people. As war chief he had a huge responsibility. Every decision he made must be a wise one.

Soon a golden crown wreathed the horizon. Warmth splashed across Touch the Clouds's face like heat from a fire. He smiled, pleased all was well with the world. His people were happy, their bellies full. Their enemies had not molested them in over a moon. Life did not get any better.

Touch the Clouds was about to go back into his lodge when moccasins pattered and around it hustled Little Grasshopper, young and lovely wife of Runs Across the River. Her eyes betrayed her state of mind, but she dutifully stopped and politely bowed her chin.

"I am sorry to disturb you, Great One. I have come to you for help."

Touch the Clouds was keenly conscious of the high esteem in which his people held him. While he was flattered, he was not fond of receiving special treatment. In truth, he was just another man. Larger than any living Shoshones, yes. Stronger than any other warrior, undeniably. But still just another man. "My heart is happy to see the wife of my friend," he said out of politeness. "How may I be of help?"

"Runs Across the River did not come back last night," Little Grasshopper divulged, and bit her lower lip.

Touch the Clouds understood her anxiety. Shoshones did not like being abroad after dark. Nighttime was when evil beings like the NunumBi were abroad. Except when on hunting trips or on raids, warriors made it a point to return to their villages by sunset. "Did your man go off hunting or to visit another village?"

"He went to visit the white men."

Touch the Clouds did not miss the bitterness in Little Grasshopper's tone. "You think he spent all night at the trading post?"

"I do not know what to think anymore. Runs Across the

David Thompson

River has gone there every day for ten sleeps. Each evening
he came home later and later. He would laugh and giggle a
lot, which is not like him. And he smelled of horse urine."

Touch the Clouds was disturbed to note tears at the corner of Little Grasshopper's eyes. It indicated how upset she
was. Crying in public was frowned on except when a loved
one died. But the references to giggling and horse urine
disturbed him even more. Winters past, back when whites
were beaver hungry, he attended several of their annual rendezvous, as the whites called them, and beheld firsthand
the effects of another substance they craved almost as
much. "Firewater," he said, one of the few English words
he knew, more to himself than to his visitor.

"I am sorry?" Little Grasshopper said in their own
tongue.

"A drink the whites are fond of," Touch the Clouds explained. "They call it 'whiskey.' Or 'firewater.' Or 'rotgut.' "

"The Crows drink it too, do they not?" Little Grasshopper said. "Why do so many use something that reeks so
awful and makes them behave like children?"

Touch the Clouds had once asked his good friend Nate
King a similar question. Nate had sighed and responded,
"People drink for different reasons. Some do it to forget
their troubles and woes. Some do it because others do.
Some because once they have a taste, they can't stop."

After witnessing how belligerent whites became after
drowning themselves in it, after beholding dozens of fist-
fights, knifings, and shootings, Touch the Clouds reached
the conclusion that firewater was yet another aspect of
white culture his people were better off without. In tribal
councils he advised against its use, warning that if the Shoshones weren't careful, they would end up like the Crows.

Among that tribe there was a saying to the effect that a
Crow who drank the white man's liquor was no longer a
Crow. Far too many of their young warriors had developed
a fondness for it, and as a result the Crows had become the

26

laughingstock of tribes far and wide. Where once they had been proud warriors, now many spent their days haunting forts and trading posts for handouts so they could buy more firewater.

"I will go look for your husband," Touch the Clouds announced.

Little Grasshopper brightened and impulsively grasped his forearm. "Would you, please? Tell him his wife and children are worried for his safety and eager for him to come home. He respects you highly and will listen to you."

"I will be back with him when the sun is there," Touch the Clouds predicted, pointing overhead. "Assure your children all will be well."

"Thank you, Great One," Little Grasshopper gushed. Beaming happily, she dipped her chin and virtually flew toward her lodge.

Touch the Clouds's features darkened. Pivoting, he hurried toward his personal horse herd, grazing an arrow's flight up the valley under the care of two of his sons. They rushed to greet him, no doubt in the mistaken belief he was going on a ride and might take one or the other along.

"Bring the sorrel," Touch the Clouds directed, and promptly wheeled. Next to his favorite warhorse—an outstanding animal he had obtained in trade with the Nez Percé—the sorrel was the fastest he possessed, and had great stamina. It could go all day and half a night without flagging.

Only one of his wives, the newest, Chickadee, was in their lodge, busy rolling up the hides they had slept on the night before. She glanced up as he marched to the peg on which his bow and quiver hung and slung them across his back.

"You are leaving us to hunt, husband?"

"I go to the white trading post," Touch the Clouds informed her. Offering no more information, he strode back out before she could badger him with questions. Unlike his other wives, she had not yet learned to tell when he did not care to discuss matters, and to hold her tongue accordingly.

Touch the Clouds did not want Runs Across the River's absence to become common knowledge. If what he suspected was true, he hoped to avoid bringing shame down on the young fool's head.

Crossing the circle, Touch the Clouds squatted in front of another lodge. "Drags the Rope? Are you in there?"

The hide parted. Tall of frame and uncommonly muscular of build, Drags the Rope straightened. A welcoming smile faded. "What is wrong, my friend?"

In hushed tones, Touch the Clouds related the little he knew, concluding with, "I would like for you to translate for me."

"As always, your wish is my wish," Drags the Rope said. "I will join you at the trees. Should I ask Shoulder Blade and some of the others to go along?"

"No," Touch the Clouds answered. The more that were asked, the more likely it was word would reach Hungry Wolf and some of the more troublesome warriors. "The two of us are sufficient."

His boys had the sorrel waiting. Distinguished by white stockings and a white blaze on its forehead, the horse stamped and snorted, raring to be off. Touch the Clouds accepted the rope reins and went to climb on.

"May we go with you, Father?" the oldest boy requested.

"Not this day."

Morning meals were under way, and few Shoshones were abroad. Those who were saw nothing unusual in his departure. A few smiled and waved.

Drags the Rope was true to his word and caught up at the tree line. The trail to the trading post on Dead Elk Creek was well-defined. Too much so, given how short a span the post had been there. They took it at a trot.

"I heard a rumor that some of our young men were spending too much time at the post," Drags the Rope commented. "Now we have proof."

"I did not hear this rumor."

"My wife told me. Among the women it is common knowledge."

"Ah. The women," Touch the Clouds said. When it pertained to village matters, the women always knew what was going on. Their fondness for gossip had a lot do with it.

They had gone only a short distance when off in the pines to their left a horse nickered. Shifting, Touch the Clouds spied a riderless bay off among the trees.

"Runs Across the River owns a horse like that," Drags the Rope said.

Touch the Clouds left the trail and cautiously drew near. It might be that his anger was unfounded. The missing warrior could have fallen prey to their many enemies, who loved to lie in wait and pick off the unwary. The last hapless victim had been a woman who went off to fill a basket with berries and was found horribly mutilated. Tracks implicated the Bloods.

A groan brought Touch the Clouds to a halt. Quickly sliding an arrow from his quiver, he notched it to his bowstring. Drags the Rope raised a lance.

The bay wearily stood staring at them, its legs and sides flecked with dust. The animal had been ridden hard, to the point of exhaustion.

A new groan sounded. This time Touch the Clouds pinpointed the source: a prone figure partially hidden in high weeds. It had to be the missing warrior. Touch the Clouds scoured the ground for sign left by a hostile war party, but there was none.

Drags the Rope was scanning the woods. "I see no one else."

"Runs Across the River, is that you?" Touch the Clouds called out.

The young warrior abruptly sat up and looked around in confusion. His hair was disheveled, his clothes splotched with dirt. "Touch the Clouds?" he said thickly. "Drags the

Rope?" Pressing a hand to his temple, he winced. "I hurt. It feels as if a bull buffalo is in my head, kicking to get out."

"You were not attacked?" Touch the Clouds inquired, slowly lowering his bow.

"Attacked?" Runs Across the River touched his face, his head. "No, I do not think so. Where am I? How did I get here?"

"You do not remember?" From Drags the Rope.

Runs Across the River pondered a moment. "The last I recall is being at the trading post. I played dice with the whites and won a cloth for Little Grasshopper." Twisting, he groped in the weeds. "Ah. Here it is." He smiled and held up a strip of red material about as long as a man's arm and twice as wide. "Isn't this pretty? She will love it."

"That she will," Touch the Clouds agreed. The women of their tribe couldn't get enough of such foofaraw, as the whites called it. Many constantly nagged their husbands for it, causing quite a few arguments and promising to cause more.

"Why can I not remember what happened after that?" Runs Across the River asked. He went to stand and involuntarily groaned. Doubling over, he gasped for air like a fish out of water and said through clenched teeth, "The pain is worse! I must be sick."

Touch the Clouds unnotched his arrow and placed it in his quiver. "Did you drink firewater while you were there?"

Runs Across the River froze. "I had a little," he reluctantly admitted.

"Do you drink it often?"

The young warrior slowly rose and took a faltering step toward his mount. "You ask a lot—" he began, and got no further. Halting, he shut his eyes and swayed like a reed in a strong wind. "The pounding!"

Touch the Clouds felt little sympathy; Runs Across the River had brought the torment on himself. "You did not answer."

"I have had a little, yes," was the defensive reply. "What of it? So do Mono and Oapiche and Meteetse and many others."

All younger men. All married, with families. Touch the Clouds intended to visit each one later, but first he had to have a talk with the whites. "Your wife is worried about you. She was afraid something had happened." He thought Runs Across the River would be touched by her devotion, but he was mistaken.

"So she went to you? That is what you are doing here?" Clenching his fists, Runs Across the River stepped to the bay. "I am a grown man. I do not need you or Drags the Rope or anyone else to look after me."

"Grown men do not leave their families alone all night," Touch the Clouds said. "What if the Piegans or the Bloods raided us while you were gone?"

The query gave Runs Across the River pause. "I see your point, and I am sorry for my hard words. Blame my headache." Grunting, he swung up. "I will go straight to my lodge and apologize to her."

"A man is truly mature when he is wise enough to admit he makes mistakes."

Runs Across the River jabbed his heels into the bay and headed for their village, still gritting his teeth.

Touch the Clouds and Drags the Rope looked at each other, then trotted in the other direction. Out of habit they traveled in silence, alert for danger. Chipmunks chattered as they passed by. Deer bounded off at their approach. To the northwest a pair of white-crowned eagles soared high in the sky.

Touch the Clouds hadn't been to the trading post since that day Artemis Borke gave him a Hawken. So he was quite taken aback when, at midday, he reached the bank of Dead Elk Creek and discovered that a log stockade now surrounded the buildings. At the southwest corner stood a tall tower in which a sentry was posted. A wide gate hung partway open.

The sentry caught sight of them right away. Leaning from the tower, he said something to someone below.

"He spoke too quietly for me to hear," Drags the Rope said.

Seconds later, to Touch the Clouds's bafflement, the gate was swung shut. A commotion broke out, a babble of voices and the thud of hooves. Drawing rein out of rifle range, he cupped a hand to his mouth and shouted, "I wish to speak to Borke." As usual, his friend translated.

Within moments the leader of the whites appeared in the tower. Laughing as if it were a great joke, he patted his ample belly and hollered, "Touch the Clouds! I didn't know it was you out there! My man mistook you for a hostile!"

Drags the Rope relayed the statement, adding suspiciously, "How can that be? Is their sentry blind?"

Touch the Clouds supposed it was possible, although unlikely. In all the mountains there wasn't another warrior anywhere, in any tribe, who came close to him in size. "We must talk, Artemis Borke!"

"Whatever you want, Chief. Just give us a minute to get things ready!"

What things? Touch the Clouds wondered. Patiently, he sat his horse while commotion issued from the post.

"They are stalling," Drags the Rope said.

But it wasn't long before the gate was flung wide and out walked Borke, as greasy and grimy as ever. Smiling, he opened his arms wide. "Come on in, my friends! You do us great honor by payin' us a visit."

The buildings were as Touch the Clouds remembered them. More than two dozen horses were now in the corral, some bearing painted symbols on their backs and flanks. Shoshone horses, several of which Touch the Clouds recognized. He stopped inside the gate and dismounted. The other whites were lounging about. To a man they were armed with rifles and a brace of pistols. "You have made some changes, Artemis Borke," he had Drags the Rope say.

Borke glanced at the stockade and the tower, and chortled. "Can you blame us? We don't want hostiles lifting our hair in the middle of the night." He clapped Touch the Clouds on the elbow. "Great to see you again, hoss. A lot of your bucks have been payin' us regular visits, but not you. How come?"

"Is that where you obtained those horses?" Touch the Clouds quizzed with a nod at the corral.

Borke showed his yellow teeth. "Sure enough. Some of your boys have animals to spare, and they've traded 'em for stuff they want. Blankets and steel knives and what have you."

"And firewater?"

Artemis Borke's smile faltered. "So that's why you're here? I reckon you and me need to palaver a bit." He pointed at the building with the crudely scrawled sign. "Why not come inside and make yourself comfortable?"

Touch the Clouds had to duck his head and shoulders to enter. The place had a musty, unclean smell. To the left a long plank rested on four large barrels. Behind it was a shelf lined with bottles of various sizes and shapes. More shelves, laden with blankets and tools and scores of trade items, filled the remaining three walls. In the center of the dirt floor were three tables ringed by chairs. On one of the tables sat a pitcher of water and several tall glasses.

"Have a seat, why don't you?" Borke invited them. "If you'd like a bite to eat, one of my men dropped a doe this mornin'. I can have a slab of roast venison and some greens whipped up quicker than you can blink."

"The water is enough." Touch the Clouds awkwardly sat down. He had used chairs only twice before and he never could fathom why whites liked them. They were stiff and uncomfortable and made his back ache if he sat in them too long. He wasn't particulary thirsty, but out of politeness he let his host fill his glass. Two other whites had followed them inside and were leaning against the plank counter.

Drags the Rope eased into his chair as gingerly as if he were sitting down on eggs.

Borke plunked down across from them. "Now, then. Something is botherin' you, Chief. I can tell. So why don't we get right to it?"

"A young man from our village did not come back last night," Touch the Clouds related. "I found him passed out in the woods." He paused. "Passed out from too much whiskey."

"I'm sorry. I truly am," Borke said with evident sincerity. "The last thing I want is to cause trouble with your people. We depend on them for the hides we need."

"Nate King told me whites no longer wear beaver fur," Touch the Clouds brought up.

Borke nodded. "And he's right, for the most part. The beaver trade ain't what it once was. But there's still a market for prime plews. Bear, wolverine, fox, buffalo, you name it, we'll trade for 'em."

Touch the Clouds scanned the shelf behind the counter. "You accept them in trade for whiskey?"

"Not on your life. We give money, just like we would to whites. Your boys have to earn their drinks like everyone else."

"I do not like firewater," Touch the Clouds declared. "It muddies a man's thoughts and makes him do things he would never do if he did not drink it."

Borke nodded in agreement. "I don't blame you. Rotgut has been the ruin of many a poor soul. Which is why I limit how much your boys can have." Rising, he went around the plank, selected a bottle and a small glass, and came back. Uncapping the bottle, he filled the small glass halfway. "That's a shot, we call it. Two of these is all your bucks can get at any one time. Then we send 'em on their merry way."

It certainly did not seem like much. Touch the Clouds

raised the small glass and examined the corn-colored liquid. The odor reminded him of the south end of northbound buffalo.

"I don't water my liquor down like some traders do. Take a swallow and see for yourself," Borke suggested.

Against his better judgment, Touch the Clouds took a sip. The firewater burned a molten path down his gullet to the pit of his stomach, and for a moment he thought he would gag. Grabbing the glass of water, he gulped enough to soothe his throat.

"Potent red-eye, ain't it?" Borke said, and snapped his fingers as if at an inspiration. "Say! Maybe that's the problem! Maybe it's too strong for 'em! With your permission, Chief, I'll start watering the whiskey down so your braves can keep their wits about 'em. What do you say?"

A pleasing warmth was spreading through Touch the Clouds's abdomen. He could see how some warriors might grow to like it. "It is a good idea. The less they drink, the less it will affect them."

A burly white over at the counter snickered and received a stern glance from Borke, who then smiled and said, "Believe you me, Chief, I only have your tribe's best interests at heart. I wouldn't let anything stand in the way of peaceful tradin' relations."

Touch the Clouds was glad the man was so accommodating. "Then we are agreed." He pushed back his chair and went to rise, but Borke thrust out a hand.

"Not so fast, if you don't mind. I'm having some trouble of my own, and I figure you're the one who can set matters straight." Borke leaned toward them. "I scratch your back, you scratch mine, eh?"

Touch the Clouds turned to Drags the Rope. "What does he mean? Why would we want to take off our shirts and scratch one another?"

"I do not know," Drags the Rope confessed. "Perhaps it

is one of those white sayings that make no sense to anyone but whites."

Borke had gone on, and Drags the Rope resumed translating. "A couple of your bucks showed up the other day. They didn't speak our language, but they made it plain they don't think much of me and my kind. One kept fingering a knife with an elk-bone handle and eyein' me like he wished he could skin me alive."

"Hungry Wolf," Touch the Clouds guessed aloud. No one else in their village owned a knife answering that description.

"He is out to turn the whites against us," Drags the Rope said. "That one was born with hatred in his blood."

"What are you two chatterin' about?" Artemis Borke asked. "Here I reckoned all your people would be right happy to have a tradin' post in their territory. Was I mistaken? Maybe me and my men should pack up and head home."

Touch the Clouds thought of how disappointed his people would be. "Do not let the act of a few influence your attitude toward the many," he had Drags the Rope say. "We are glad you are here and hope you will stay for many winters to come."

"How long that will be depends on your people," Borke said. "So long as they treat us decent and bring us items for trade, we'll be tickled to oblige. But keep that buck with the bone-handled knife away from the post, or he's liable to spoil it for everyone."

"I will have words with him," Touch the Clouds promised. Although it might do little good. He was a leader, yes, but his word was not law, as whites phrased it. Every Shoshone was free to do as he saw fit, provided his actions did not cause harm to the tribe.

"I can't ask for more, Chief." Borke reached across and shook Touch the Clouds's hand. "You'd do to ride the river with."

Again Touch the Clouds was perplexed. "Ride on the river or beside it?" he said to Drags the Rope. "Horses cannot walk on water."

At a gesture from Borke, one of the other whites brought over a pair of Mackinaw blankets and deposited them on the table. "One for each of you," Borke said, beaming, "as a token of our thanks."

Touch the Clouds would refuse were it not for his wives and their fondness for new things. Draping the blanket over his left arm, he held his head high as the whites escorted them to their horses.

"Pay us a visit anytime," Borke said in parting. "Bring the family and we'll treat 'em all to gifts."

"That went well," Drags the Rope commented as they cantered toward the creek.

Touch the Clouds tended to agree. But it bothered him slightly that lusty mirth pealed from the post moments after they passed through the gate.

Chapter Three

As the mountaion lion sprang, cleaving the air in a graceful arc, Nate King yanked his tomahawk from under his wide leather belt. The cougar didn't quite reach him, though. It landed several feet away and crouched low, its tail snapping back and forth. Growling, it bared its razor fangs.

Nate braced for the inevitable rush. He had always known that one day this might happen. The wilderness was rife with threats to life and limb, and frontiersmen daily lived with the prospect of horribly violent deaths. It was part and parcel of their existence, and they learned to take it in stride. Still, given his druthers, Nate would have liked to die quietly in bed with his family by his side to comfort his soul in its passage from this world to the bosom of his Maker.

Nate had read the Bible from cover to cover. Back in his trapping days, on those long winter nights when snowdrifts ten feet high socked the trappers in their dingy cabins with little else to do, he had read anything and everything he could get his hands on. The fictional works of James Fenimore Cooper. The plays of Shakespeare. Poetry. And the Good Book. He couldn't claim to understand all of it. But he did come to believe there definitely was a God, and if a person had faith, however feeble, then they were destined to live on beyond their mortal coil.

Nate mentally clutched at that now, like a drowning man clutching at a log. He would die, but he would live on. What lay beyond the veil, he couldn't rightly say. No one could. But there had to be something. There just *had* to.

Images of Winona, Evelyn, Zach, and Louisa floated before him, and Nate's chest grew heavy and tight. He would miss them, miss them unbearably. His family was everything to him. He took great pride in the fact that whatever else he had done, however many blunders he had made, he had always striven the best he knew how to be the best husband and father he could be.

The cougar growled again. Keeping one eye on him, it inched to the black bear and sniffed the body.

Nate scarcely breathed. His musings on death had been premature. He might yet live, if all the cat was interested in was the bear.

The mountain lion sank its teeth into the bruin's neck. Planting all four paws, it attempted to drag the heavy bulk toward the coulee entrance. Mountain lions were immensely strong and could partially lift fair-sized deer in their powerful jaws, but the bear outweighed a typical deer by hundreds of pounds. The painter had dragged it only a few yards when the cat halted, panting and hissing.

"Try again," Nate coaxed. Better for him if the cougar went elsewhere. The longer it stuck around, the more tempted it might be to take a bite out of him.

The mountain lion swiveled toward him. Its fierce eyes narrowing, it dipped its belly to the ground and crept toward him, its intention transparent. It had changed its mind about the bear and was after live prey.

Nate raised his tomahawk. The brief rest had done him some good, and while he was still woozy, he had regained enough strength that he thought he could stand. His back against the wall, he started pushing himself up.

The cougar halted, its tail darting like a bullwhip.

"Get out of here!" Nate hollered, seeking to bluff it into fleeing. But no such luck.

Ears flat, lips pulled back over its tapered teeth, the painter continued stalking him. Another second or two and it would spring.

Then the unforeseen occurred.

From the mouth of the coulee came a cry of "Pa!" The mountain lion hesitated; for a moment it appeared the cat would turn and flee.

"Evelyn?" Nate answered, and inadvertently incited the painter into launching itself at him. Almost too late, Nate swung the tomahawk. It struck the cat a glancing blow with just enough force to knock it down but not enough to kill it.

The effort proved costly. Nate's newfound strength drained from him with startling rapidity. He sought to raise the tomahawk again, but his head was spinning and his arms were leaden.

Growling horribly, the cougar crouched for another try.

Fear flooded through Nate—fear for his daughter, not for himself. Should she come rushing around the bend, the cat might turn on her instead. Getting his legs under him, he lurched toward it, swinging wildly, weakly. The cat rushed head-on, its front paws flashing, clawed lightning in feline form. Nate reeled from a sweeping slash to the chest. Another second and he was flat on his back with the cougar's front paws on his sternum and its jaws descending toward his throat. His vision blurred, and for that he was grateful. He tensed for the searing sensation of his neck being ripped apart. Darkness enclosed him, and he seemed to pitch into a great inky void. Dimly, he heard thunder, and a screech, and after that, he heard and felt nothing at all.

Winona King had learned long ago to trust her intuition. Like many women, she became aware of certain special feelings when she was quite young. An urge to do something would come over her, an urge so strong, denying it was impossible.

Once, when Winona had barely seen ten winters, she was out gathering firewood with a couple of other girls when she felt danger was near. She experienced an impulse to hide, and hide quickly. She told her friends, but they gazed at the sunny sky and the bright forest and they scoffed at her silliness. There was nothing to fear, they said, and walked on without her.

Winona had begun to follow, but the feeling became stronger. Confused, torn between her strange, inexplicable terror and common sense, she had compromised and darted behind a spruce tree. A stifled scream changed her blood to ice. Not twenty paces away, half a dozen painted shadows had detached themselves from the vegetation and pounced on her friends. It was a Piegan raiding party. Their brawny hands clamped over the mouths of her friends, the Piegans retreated into the woods as soundlessly as they had come.

Winona's heart had pounded in her young breast. She was sure the Piegans had seen her and would grab her next. But no, they faded into the distance, and marshaling her courage, she flew to the village to spread the alarm. Warriors poured into the woods to rescue the two girls. They chased the Piegans for sleeps on end, but the wily raiders eluded them and the two girls were never seen again.

The incident was the first inkling Winona had that she possessed an amazing inner power, a sense that defied reason yet the reality of which could not be denied. She had discussed it with her mother and learned that many women, and quite a few men, also possessed it. No one could explain exactly how the strange sense worked, only that those who ignored it did so at their own peril.

Another time, fifteen winters along, Winona was on her way to a spot on the Green River favored by the women for washing clothes. Her intuition halted her in her tracks. She had a feeling that she must get off the trail right that instant. Feeling slightly silly, she darted behind a thicket.

That was when a massive grizzly appeared. Lumbering up the very same trail, it came to the exact spot where she had been standing and sniffed loudly, its nose to the ground. It had caught her scent.

Quaking in uncontrollable fright, Winona was debating whether to sneak off toward the village when the giant bear reared onto its hind legs and stared at her over the top of the thicket. Her own legs wobbled, and she came close to fainting. Grizzlies were indestructible monsters that had taken many a Shoshone life, and hers was about to be counted among them. She couldn't possibly outrun it even if she could compel her legs to work.

For an eternity the bear stared. Then it dropped onto all fours, snorted, wheeled, and padded off into the woodland, leaving an astounded Winona in its wake. More incidents were to occur, establishing beyond any shred of doubt that denying her intuition was tantamount to stupidity.

So it was that on this bright and carefree morning, as Winona puttered around her cabin cleaning up after the morning meal and making the bed, she became greatly upset when a familiar feeling came over her. A feeling of imminent danger. Only, the danger wasn't to herself. She clearly felt that her husband and her daughter needed her, needed her badly, and she must reach them swiftly, without delay.

Going to the cabin door, Winona scanned the trail to the lake. The last she had seen of them was when she watched from the window as her daughter raced to catch up to her husband. She listened but heard nothing to indicate they were in any trouble. Still, the feeling persisted.

From pegs on the wall Winona took her ammunition pouch and powder horn and slung them across her chest. Her Hawken, always loaded and primed, was propped against the wall. Grasping it, and helping herself to a pistol from over the hearth, she hastened across the clearing.

"Nate?" Winona called, and received no response. Her sense of inner urgency mounted. She ran down to the lakeshore and jogged down to the water, but they were nowhere to be seen. "Blue Flower?" she shouted, using her daughter's Shoshone name. "Where are you?"

Out on the water a duck quacked, and from nearby brush several sparrows took swift wing. Other than that, the valley was still and silent.

Winona bent to the ground. The soil was soft enough that she could read their tracks. Blue Flower had caught up with Nate and together they had hiked around the lake toward the east end. Winona also saw fresh bear tracks and surmised what her husband was up to. She hurried after them, pacing herself so she would not tire too soon.

The tracks were those of a black bear. Since her husband had slain more grizzlies than any man living or dead, red or white, she saw no reason to be unduly concerned. He could kill a black bear with one hand tied behind his back, as white men liked to say.

Why, then, was her intuition urging her to go faster?

Winona came to where her loved ones had gone into the forest. Low limbs and brush tore at her beaded buckskin dress, but she paid them no heed. Leaping a shredded log, she paralleled their tracks toward a high ridge and increased her speed. The feeling that something was amiss, that something dreadful was about to occur or had occurred, was so potent it was almost paralyzing.

"Nate? Blue Flower?" Winona yelled. Where *were* they? Why didn't they answer? Surely they could hear her?

Winona was flying now, her moccasins slapping the earth as swiftly as the beat of a hummingbird's wings. The Hawken was heavy in her hand, and she firmed her hold. "Nate? Nate?"

"Ma?"

The reply slowed Winona to a brisk walk. "Blue Flower?" She looked right and left, seeking to pinpoint the direction the cry came from.

"Ma! This way! Hurry! Pa's hurt!"

Winona raced on. A branch nearly speared her eye, but she didn't care. An inner voice was shrieking for her to run as she had never run before. Her mate needed her and she wouldn't let anything keep her from him. "Blue Flower? Where are you?"

"Over here, Ma!"

Evelyn materialized out of the undergrowth so abruptly, they nearly collided. Grabbing hold of Winona's left hand, she pulled Winona toward the ridge. "The bear got him, Ma! It got him bad!"

"A black bear?" Winona said in stunned disbelief.

"It ripped Pa up," Evelyn clarified, "and he's bleeding something awful." She motioned at a steep-sided coulee ahead. "In there."

Winona pulled loose and sprinted into the coulee. She hadn't gone five strides when she heard a feral snarl from the shadowed depths before her. *The bear must still be alive.* Cocking the Hawken, she rounded a bend. The snarling grew louder. She wedged the rifle to her shoulder and moments later burst onto a scene birthed in her worst nightmare. Her husband was on his back, bleeding profusely from a dozen wounds. Over him stood not a black bear, but a mountain lion, its fearsome maw about to clamp onto Nate's jugular.

"No!" Winona cried.

The cougar whirled. A living embodiment of elemental ferocity, it leaped off Nate and came at her in a blur of claws and fur.

Winona stroked her rifle's trigger and the Hawken

boomed like thunder in the narrow confines, belching lead and smoke. The impact of the slug punched the mountain lion onto its haunches. But not for long. Venting a bestial shriek, it streaked toward her again in a fit of raw fury.

Her Hawken was empty, but Winona still had the pistol. She flashed it up and out, thumbing back the hammer as she extended her arm, and fired just as the mountain lion sprang. At virtual arm's length she shot it between the eyes.

The cat executed an aerial flip and smashed onto its belly. Seemingly unfazed, it began to rise, but it had risen only a few inches when its legs buckled and it sank down with a strangled hiss, blood and brains seeping from the bullet hole.

"Nate?" Winona rushed to her man's side. Anguish seared her heart at the horrid spectacle he presented. He had suffered a terrible wound on his forehead, and a flap of skin hung over one eye. His shoulder had been bitten down to the bone. His shirt was in tatters, pink flesh showing underneath where the cougar's claws had sliced, and his leggings were in little better condition. Everywhere there was blood. So much blood.

Winona prided herself on her self-control, but she couldn't suppress the tears that filled her eyes or stop her stomach from churning. "Husband," she said softly, tenderly touching his chin. "My darling, dearest husband."

"Ma, what do we do?" Evelyn had come up unnoticed and was gawking in absolute horror at the ghastly apparition that a mere half hour before had epitomized vitality and endurance.

"We get him home," Winona said.

"But how? He's too heavy for us to carry."

That he was. As a lark, Nate had weighed himself once on a visit to St. Louis and pegged the scale at two hundred and fifty-seven pounds, all muscle and bone. Winona had no illusions about being able to tote him to the cabin unaided. "One of us must go for my mare, a rope, and an ax. The other must stay and guard him."

Without hesitation, Evelyn said, "I'll stay. You run faster than me and can get back that much sooner."

Winona was loath to leave them, but it had to be done. Rising, she swept both sides of the coulee from bottom to top, verifying that there were no other imminent threats. "Is your rifle loaded?"

"No," Evelyn said a shade sheepishly.

"What has your father taught you about that?"

"To always reload the first chance I get," Evelyn recited. "But all I could think of was bringing you."

"Reload now," Winona instructed, and did the same herself, first her Hawken, then her pistol. She knew exactly how much black powder to pour in without having to measure it. The balls and patches were next. Then she tamped the bullets down with their respective ramrods. "Here." She handed the pistol to her daughter, butt first. "Just in case."

Evelyn nodded. "Hurry on back, you hear?"

"I will fly like the wind," Winona promised, and was true to her word. She ran flat out, out the coulee and down the short slope to the forest and on through the dense trees to the lake. Her legs protested, but she didn't care.

At the cabin Winona quickly gathered up a coil of rope and an ax, and led her mare from the corral. She didn't bother with a saddle. Since she couldn't carry her rifle and the ax, both, she left the Hawken indoors. Sliding the rope over her left shoulder, she clambered on, gripped the mare's mane, and was off.

It had been years since Winona rode bareback. Fond memories of her childhood surfaced, but she smothered them and focused on reaching the coulee with all deliberate haste. None of Nate's wounds appeared to be life-threatening in and of themselves, but the loss of blood worried her. So did the risk of infection. It was a little-known fact that more people died of infection from animal attacks than from the attacks themselves. She needed to clean him and get him bandaged as soon as possible.

The mare had not been ridden in a while and was glad to be given her head. Fleet and surefooted, she covered the distance in a tenth of the time it had taken on foot.

Near a stand of saplings close to the coulee Winona brought her mount to a stop. She vaulted down, selected a slender bole, and chopped at it in a frenzy of worry. Chips flew fast and furious, and soon there came a rending *crack*. The sapling keeled earthward. Winona chopped down four more in rapid succession. Trimming the branches took only a couple of minutes.

Winona set about fashioning a travois. Used by various tribes, it was a means of transporting everything from lodges to clothes to kids. She lashed two poles together in an inverted V shape, then applied cross-braces. Ordinarily, a hide was spread over the braces for extra support, but she didn't have the time.

Attaching the travois to the mare was simple. Winona dragged it over behind the horse, arranging it so the narrow end was to the mare. To hold it on, she cut several lengths of rope and tied one end of each to the right pole and the other end to the left. By leaving enough slack, she was able to fit the ropes snugly over the mare's back. Lastly, she looped yet another rope around the animal's neck and knotted it to the outer poles.

Her work done, Winona swung on. Her weight was added insurance that the travois wouldn't slide loose. Chafing to reach Nate, she prodded the mare toward the coulee, the travois dragging behind them.

Evelyn was hunkered beside her father, her face twisted in misery. "He's hardly breathing, Ma. I can't get him to open his eyes or anything."

One glance and Winona couldn't resist a shiver of apprehension. Her mate was as pale as a sheet and as motionless as a rock slab. Terror nipping at her heart, Winona knelt and placed an ear to his chest. A beat pulsed, oh so faintly, telling her he was still alive.

"We must get him out of here," Winona said, stating the obvious, and moved around to slide her hands under his armpits. "I have a travois waiting."

"I can help."

Winona surged upward but succeeded only in raising Nate's head and shoulders off the ground. "Lend a hand, daughter. We must drag him."

They strained. They pulled. They heaved. The best they could do was a turtle's pace. They had to stop frequently to catch their breaths. Winona was exasperated by the delay. Every moment spent increased the likelihood of infection setting in.

After an eternity they reached the opening. But worse lay before them. They had to drag him a short distance yet, over sharp rocks, and hoist him up. The first part they accomplished, but the second defied them. Each time they tried to lift him, gravity thwarted their attempt. They could get him partway up, but their arms always gave out and they had to set him down again before they dropped him.

"It's like trying to lift our cabin," Evelyn complained.

Winona had an idea. They dragged Nate to a small earthen hump and laid him lengthwise on top. Mounting the mare, she brought it over and aligned the travois, lengthwise, so that all they had to do was roll Nate onto it.

Riding double, they made a beeline for the cabin. Or tried to. Logs and boulders and trees necessitated constant detours, continual delays. It didn't help any that they had to hold to a walk for fear of jostling Nate too severely.

Over an hour after they set out, Winona halted the mare near their front door. How to get Nate inside was another problem. Winona wasn't fond of the idea of dragging him over the doorstep. As she stood there mulling it over, she remembered how Nate carried heavy objects when need be, and she figured she would try his technique. Squatting at the broad end of the travois, she gripped him by the front of his shirt and slowly pulled him toward her. By bending the upper half of her body, she was able to drape him across her.

"You're not fixing to try what I think you're fixing to try, are you, Ma?" Evelyn anxiously asked.

"Do you have a better idea?" Winona rejoined. Bracing herself, she adjusted Nate's weight evenly across her shoulders and slowly straightened. Her knees crackled in protest and her legs quivered. For a few harrowing moments she thought they would buckle, but they didn't. Slightly stooped over, Winona paused to take a few deep breaths and gather her strength. It truly did feel as if she had the cabin resting on her shoulders, and she was unsure whether she could make it inside.

"Is there anything I can do, Ma?"

"Hold the door open," Winona said. Her daughter scooted to obey, and Winona gingerly slid her right foot toward the doorway. She did the same with her left. In that manner, inches at a time, she reached the doorstep, which was a hand's width higher than the ground. Exercising exquisite care, she eased her right foot high enough to place it flat on the floorboards. Now came the moment of truth. Winona applied their combined weight to her right leg and lifted her left foot. It put her momentarily off balance. Frightened of losing her balance, she flung her hands at the jambs for support, gripped hard, and pulled.

It worked, but not as she had hoped.

Winona stumbled inside. She got both feet under her but tottered wildly. Without warning Nate shifted, and the added pressure bent her nearly in half. She couldn't see where she was going.

Evelyn yelled a warning. Before Winona could stop, she staggered against a chair and her left leg was bumped out from under her. "No!" she cried as she pitched forward, crashing into their table. It upended under them.

49

Winona lost her grip on Nate and they went down in a whirl of human limbs and table legs. Her shoulder bore the brunt, and she rolled, unharmed except for a pang in her side. Nate wasn't as fortunate. His chest cracked into the edge of the table and he was catapulted head over heels, striking the floor with a loud thud.

Her heart in her throat, Winona scrambled over and eased him onto his back. It was impossible to tell if the fall had hurt him internally, but fresh drops of blood speckled his lower lip and he had a nasty scrape on his left cheek.

Evelyn was glued in shock.

"Help me," Winona said. Together, they dragged Nate to the big bed. Together, they elevated him by gradual degrees until they had him spread-eagle on the quilt. "We need hot water, daughter. Lots and lots of hot water. Run to the lake and fill the bucket while I start a fire."

"Will do, Ma." Evelyn was out the door in a twinkling.

Collecting logs from a stack near their fireplace, Winona knelt in front of it and placed them on top of the charred coals from their last fire. She added kindling from a special box on a small shelf above the hearth, then used a fire steel and flint to ignite it. Once the sparks had produced a tiny flame, she delicately puffed until larger flames licked the wood.

Undressing Nate was next. Winona tugged his moccasins off and removed his belt and pants. The gashes in his legs were horrible, but nothing compared to his chest, shoulder, and forehead. Angry at the cruel caprice of fate that had stricken the one she loved, she tossed his crumpled, bloody shirt into a corner.

"You will not die on me, husband!" Winona declared. "I will not let you." Bending down, she kissed his cheek—and recoiled in alarm. He was burning hot to the touch. She placed a palm on his forehead, confirming that a raging fever had claimed him. Not only that, the flesh where his scalp had been torn was becoming discolored. It could only mean one thing.

Infection had set in.

Chapter Four

Several tranquil days passed, and all was well in the Shoshone village. Small boys played with small bows and knives, honing their skills for the day they would become grown warriors. Small girls played with dolls made of supple buffalo hide stuffed with soft grass. Women busied themselves at a variety of daily tasks—cooking, cleaning, mending garments, sewing new ones. The men had bow strings to make and lances to sharpen, games of chance to play, and items of import to discuss around the fire at night.

Life was good. The Shoshones were content. Which pleased Touch the Clouds to no end. He took his responsibility as leader in earnest and placed their welfare before all else.

On a sunny afternoon with a light wind blowing from the west, Touch the Clouds stood near his lodge watching five boys stalk a "buffalo" they had constructed from dead branches and an old, discarded hide. He smiled at their antics. It brought back the sweet savor of his own youth, and he sighed with wistful longing.

"I am sorry to disturb you."

Touch the Clouds's fond remembrance dissolved and he turned to find Drags the Rope approaching. With his friend came Little Grasshopper, her head bowed, her cheeks damp. "What is wrong, my brother?"

"I was walking by their lodge and heard her crying," Drags the Rope revealed. "Runs Across the River did not come back again last night."

"Again?" Anger flowered. Touch the Clouds thought the young warrior had learned his lesson the last time. "Did he go to the trading post?"

Little Grasshopper sniffled and looked up. "He would not tell me where he was going, but that is where I think he went. He took our best bear hide, the one our children sleep on, and a necklace my mother gave me."

"Why would he—?" Touch the Clouds stopped. The answer lay in the liquor bottles lined up behind the counter at the post. "We will bring him back for you, Little Grasshopper. But this time his behavior cannot be excused." He frowned. "You should have come to me sooner."

"I did not want him to get into trouble," Little Grasshopper said contritely. "I did not want the Logs to hear of it."

Like other tribes, the Shoshones were divided into several societies, the Logs and the Yellow Noses prominent among them. The Yellow Noses were elite warriors who excelled in battle. The Logs were responsible for keeping order in camp, which included punishing offenders who committed acts detrimental to village welfare. Nate King once told Touch the Clouds that the Logs were the Shoshone equivalent of white police.

Little Grasshopper clasped her hands in appeal. "Please, Great One. For my husband's sake, and for the sake of my family, please do not inform the Logs. They might whip him. Or take away his horses and his weapons."

It would serve him right, Touch the Clouds wanted to say, but he didn't. "Your husband is thoughtless and immature. He disrupts the harmony of your family. Left on his own, he could disrupt the harmony of our entire band. This I cannot allow."

Crestfallen, Little Grasshopper walked off.

"I will get my horse and join you," Drags the Rope said. Taking a step, he paused. "Only the two of us?"

"Pick ten warriors. The whites are as much to blame as Runs Across the River. We will confront their leader and demand they stop selling firewater permanently."

In the time it would take a pipe to be smoked, the group was mounted and gathered in front of Touch the Clouds's dwelling. As Touch the Clouds stepped out into the sunlight, his quiver strapped to his back, he beheld dozens of men and women converging from all over. Word had spread that something unusual was taking place.

Foremost among those gathering was Hungry Wolf, his lean features pinched in distrust. "Where are all of you off to?" he demanded. "Are there enemies in the area the rest of us do not know about?"

"I go to speak with the whites," Touch the Clouds divulged. He would say no more. The hothead would want to rise up in force and wipe the whites out.

"What about?" Hungry Wolf asked. With him were Buffalo Hump and Wallowing Bull. Both just as young. Both as spiteful toward whites.

"Trade," Touch the Clouds said. Which was true in one respect. Vaulting astride the sorrel, he led his group to the trail. They had covered five times the distance a strong bow could shoot an arrow when hooves pounded and five more warriors overtook them, Hungry Wolf out in front.

"We decided to come along."

Touch the Clouds did not like it, but he had no right to refuse them. He couldn't command them to go back. As full-fledged warriors, they were free to do as they desired, even if their wills conflicted with his, or with the will of any Shoshone leader.

Long ago Nate King had informed Touch the Clouds that in white society it was different. In the white world, their chiefs were given power to boss others around as they saw fit. The whites, evidently, were not as free as they believed themselves to be.

No Shoshone would tolerate being ordered about. Tribal leaders and war chiefs could propose plans of action and make recommendations in council, but no one was obligated to do as they advised. To Touch the Clouds's way of thinking, his people enjoyed a purer form of freedom than the whites. A freedom that now came back to haunt him.

"Come if you wish," Touch the Clouds said, "but do not interfere. Drags the Rope will translate for the rest of us."

Hungry Wolf snickered. "Let him flap his lips until they fall off, if he wants. I do not speak the white tongue anyway."

Touch the Clouds lashed his sorrel with his quirt and was soon out ahead of the rest, except for Drags the Rope.

"Hungry Wolf is not to be trusted," his friend remarked. "He will make trouble for us if given the chance."

"Then we must be certain not to give him that chance," Touch the Clouds said.

Steady riding brought them to a long, grassy valley where the Shoshones occasionally grazed their horses. Drags the Rope, whose eyesight had always been keener, gestured. "There! At the other end of the valley. Do you see them?"

Shielding his eyes from the sun's harsh glare, Touch the Clouds spotted a pair of walking figures. Or perhaps "weaving" figures would be more accurate, for as he watched, they wove from side to side like young bears not used to moving on their hind legs.

"Can it be?" Drags the Rope said.

Grimly, Touch the Clouds galloped across the valley. He

was a rifle shot from the pair when strident singing fell on his ears, and tittering such as women voiced when in fine spirits. But the two weaving figures weren't women.

Arms across each other's shoulders, Runs Across the River and Bear's Backbone were oblivious to the world around them. They giggled hysterically when Runs Across the River nearly tripped over his own feet.

Touch the Clouds reined up directly in their path. They were practically close enough to touch the sorrel's muzzle before Runs Across the River glanced up, blinked in consternation, then broke out in a broad grin.

"Look who it is, Bear's Backbone! Our friends are here to see us safely home!"

The young warrior's words were slurred, his eyes bloodshot and glazed. They both reeked of firewater, and Bear's Backbone's leggings were stained from his crotch to his knees.

"I hope you brought extra horses," Runs Across the River said. "We have misplaced ours." At that, the pair cackled inanely.

Drags the Rope and the other warriors spread out in a semicircle, their disgust boundless. "What have you done to yourselves?" one asked.

Runs Across the River stiffened and squared his shoulders. "We had a few glasses of firewater at the trading post. So what?"

"So you have been away from your family all night again," Touch the Clouds interposed. He swept his gaze to the far horizon and back again. "Where are your horses? Did they run off on you? Or did you forget them and leave them at the post?"

"We left them there," Bear's Backbone sniggered, "but we did not forget them."

"Explain," Touch the Clouds said.

"We cannot. It is a secret." Chortling, Runs Across the River covered his mouth with his hand.

"We promised him we would not tell anyone," Bear's Backbone said, and both succumbed to another fit of giggling.

Hungry Wolf was scowling and fingering his quirt as if he dearly yearned to apply it to their backs. "Have the two of you lost your senses? Have you no shame?" Bending toward them, he sniffed a few times. "What is that stink?"

Touch the Clouds smelled it, too. The unmistakable odor of alcohol. For the stench to be so strong, the two young warriors had to ingest a large amount. "This is a serious situation—" he began, only to spark a series of hoots and guffaws.

Drags the Rope's features were like the crags of a rocky cliff. "They behave like children who have not yet seen four winters," he voiced his disgust.

Runs Across the River stood straighter. "We are fine!" he huffed. "Go away and leave us be."

"And if a Blackfoot or Crow war party should come across you?" Touch the Clouds rebutted. "You are not in any condition to defend yourselves. They would torture you at their leisure, then lift your hair."

"We are fine, I tell you!"

"Where is the necklace given to Little Grasshopper by her mother?" Touch the Clouds inquired.

"What?" Runs Across the River's mouth grew slack with surprise.

"And the fine bear hide your girls sleep on?"

"Who told you about them?" Runs Across the River snapped, a crimson tinge spreading up his neck and face to his hairline. "My wife! She must have!" He ground his teeth together in suppressed fury. "Waugh! Women can never keep their tongues from wagging when they should not."

"You traded the necklace and the hide to the whites," Touch the Clouds said. "You traded them, and your horses, for money to buy firewater."

Both young warriors reacted as if they had been slapped.

"Who are you to question us like this?" Bear's Backbone demanded.

"We are grown men and can do as we please," Runs Across the River added. "What we do with our possessions is none of your concern."

"It is when it disrupts the harmony of our village."

"That shows how much you know. We are not even *at* the village." In his befuddled state, Runs Across the River did not realize his logic was no logic at all. "Go pester someone else. We were enjoying ourselves until you came along."

Bear's Backbone took a step. "Snooping into our private affairs! You are worse than old women, the whole bunch of you!"

A snarl rose from Hungry Wolf, and with a slap of his muscular legs he brought his horse alongside the pair. "How dare you!" His arm blurred, and he laid his quirt squarely across Bear's Backbone's cheek. The young warrior staggered and would have fallen had Runs Across the River not clumsily clutched hold of him. "Insult us again and I will use more than my quirt!"

Bear's Backbone lowered his left hand to a knife on his hip.

"Enough!" Touch the Clouds shouted. The young fool was on the verge of committing a cardinal breach of Shoshone custom. For one Shoshone to slay another was considered heinous, and was punished with the utmost severity. "We are riding to the trading post, and the two of you are coming with us."

The pair still did not appreciate the seriousness of their behavior. "Who are you to tell us what we must do?" Runs Across the River huffed. "Go to the post if you want, but we are not going along." He started to shuffle past the sorrel, Bear's Backbone trudging sullenly along.

"Let them do as they see fit," Drags the Rope said. "Some men only learn lessons the hard way."

"I agree," Hungry Wolf stated. "But they are not entirely

at fault. The whites are as much to blame, if not more. This would not have happened if they had not set up their trading post."

Touch the Clouds did not say anything, but the white-hater had a valid point. The traders should not have let Runs Across the River and Bear's Backbone drink so much. Artemis Borke had promised him something like this would never occur, yet it had. Borke had broken his promise. "We will go on without them," he decided.

The remainder of the ride was conducted in tense silence. At Dead Elk Creek they came to a halt and were seen by the sentry in the tall tower, who immediately yelled to the other whites below.

"He says for someone to run and tell Borke we are here," Drags the Rope translated. "Do we wait for them to come out to greet us?"

"We do not." Touch the Clouds trotted toward the open gate. The whites might not like having a large party of armed warriors enter their compound, but that was too bad. Surprisingly, though, the sentry grinned and waved as if they were the best of friends, and no sooner had he drawn rein inside the palisade than Artemis Borke came hastening toward him, all smiles.

"Touch the Clouds! This is a pleasant surprise. You don't visit us near often enough." Borke offered his hand, and when Touch the Clouds merely sat there, he glanced at each of the Shoshones in turn. "What's the matter? You coons look as if the Bloods just wiped out half your tribe."

"We are displeased," Drags the Rope relayed from Touch the Clouds. "You have spoken with two tongues and lost our trust."

Borke appeared bewildered by the allegation. "When have I ever lied to you? What's this all about, anyhow?" He paused. "It wouldn't have anything to do with those two bucks who swiped a bottle of my best whiskey, would it?

You can't blame me for that. I trust your people. I gave them the run of the post."

"Are you saying that Runs Across the River and Bear's Backbone stole firewater?" The allegation stunned Touch the Clouds.

"Was that their names?" Artemis Borke adopted a pained expression. "I'm real sorry to break the news. I was hopin' nothing would come of it. I don't want any of your people gettin' into trouble on our account."

"You did not sell them the firewater?"

"Just two drinks apiece, like I promised. But it wasn't enough. They demanded more. When Orley, the man who was servin' them, refused, they got all riled and stalked out. He figured that was the end of it. But when he was over in a corner stackin' merchandise, one of 'em snuck back in and took a bottle right off the shelf. Orley saw him as the buck ran out the door. They were out the gate before anyone could stop them." Borke sadly shook his head. "Hell, they were in such a hurry they left their horses here."

"They did not sell their horses?"

Borke was offended. "What do you take me for? I gave you my word I wouldn't sell more than two drinks to every warrior who comes here, remember?"

Hungry Wolf listened to the exchange with rising impatience. "So what if the white cur speaks with a straight tongue? He and the rest must be held responsible. They sell the firewater. They brought the temptation."

Drags the Rope did not translate, and Artemis Borke uneasily shifted his weight from one boot to the other.

"I don't rightly know what that hoss said, but from the sound of things he's madder than a wet hen. I appeal to you, Touch the Clouds. Be reasonable. It was those two young bucks who wouldn't do as we agreed. I've been true to my word."

Among his people Touch the Clouds was highly regarded for his ability to listen to both sides of a dispute and render impartial and just suggestions for resolving them. Now that he had heard the white version of events, he was torn between his sense of responsibility to his people and his sense of justice.

"Why do you sit there with your mouth shut?" Hungry Wolf challenged. "Tell these worms we do not want them in our territory. Tell them to pack up and leave before we drive them off."

"If they have kept their word, then it is we who are in the wrong," Touch the Clouds said.

"Right. Wrong. What does it matter? The important thing is for the whites to leave."

"Since when is it honorable for the Shoshones to treat others with less respect than we are treated in turn? These whites came to us with their arms wide in friendship. We granted them the right to stay so long as they did as we asked. To drive them off now would be a sign to all their kind that we are the ones who speak with two tongues."

Hungry Wolf angrily wagged his quirt. "Why should we care how the whites regard us? What have they ever done for our people to deserve our friendship? Have they sided with us in our dispute with the Crows? Have they given us guns with which to fight the Piegans and the Bloods? I have yet to meet a white who is worth a gourd of horse piss."

"Does that include Grizzly Killer?" Touch the Clouds asked.

"Do not try to put words in my mouth. I know he is your blood brother. And I am willing to concede that of all the whites I have met, he is the only one I respect." Hungry Wolf encompassed the trading post with a sweep of his arm. "Now, you must concede that these whites are not like him. They have not taken up our ways. They have not been formally adopted into our tribe."

"You are being unreasonable," Touch the Clouds responded. "We cannot adopt every white we meet. We cannot expect all of them to live as we do when they have ways of their own. Grizzly Killer is an exception. He has the heart of a red man in a white body."

Artemis Borke chose that moment to interject, "What's all the jawin' about? If it concerns me and my boys, have the courtesy to let me know. I swear to God, we only want what's best for all of us."

Touch the Clouds turned. "Would you object if we asked to take the two horses that were left behind?"

"Help yourselves," Borke said. "Hell, if it'll help patch things up, you're welcome to the bear hide and the necklace one of those young bucks traded. They're not worth spoilin' our friendship over."

The offer was unforeseen. Touch the Clouds was all too familiar with the value whites placed on possessions. "I commend your kindness. I will be sure to mention it to all my people at our next council."

Borke sent a hawk-faced man to fetch the horses and other items.

"We are making a mistake," Hungry Wolf asserted. "We should drive them out now, or in six moons half the men in our village will be addicted to firewater."

"So long as the whites keep their word, we will keep ours," Touch the Clouds vowed.

Hungry Wolf and his friends did not like it, did not like it one bit, but they didn't object or interfere when the horses were led over. Drags the Rope accepted the lead rope. Touch the Clouds accepted the hide and the necklace.

"Are you sure I can't talk you into stayin' a spell?" Artemis Borke asked as the Shoshones prepared to leave.

"Another day," Touch the Clouds said.

"So you keep sayin'. Oh well. The important thing is, we're still pards."

Touch the Clouds wheeled his sorrel and the rest of the Shoshones trailed him out the gate. He was troubled. Part of him believed he had done the right thing; another part of him felt he might have just made one of the worst mistakes of his life.

The drum of hoofbeats faded in the distance and the hawk-visaged man, whose handle was Orley, pivoted toward Artemis Borke. "What in hell did you go and do that for? Those horses were prime horseflesh. And that turquoise necklace would fetch fifty dollars or better."

"He's got a point," chimed in Peck Danton. "You just threw a fistful of good money away."

Borke sighed and arched an eyebrow at his companions. "How many times must I explain how things are? How long before you yaks get it through your thick skulls? For this to work, we have to bend a tad at times. It'll pay off in the long run."

"So you keep saying," Orley muttered.

"I'm surrounded by idiots," Borke said, and headed for their living quarters. In his estimation it was extremely unfortunate he couldn't pull this off alone. Having to share the take with eight others left that much less for him. And the whole scheme was his brainstorm. By rights, he was the one who deserved to benefit the most.

A white-haired old geezer by the name of Shakespeare McNair was largely responsible for kindling Borke's brainstorm. About ten months before, McNair had paid a visit to Borke's store in St. Louis, the Mercantile Emporium. It specialized in all sorts of gear and provisions for those bound for the frontier. McNair bought ammo and a skinning knife, and at one point noticed a fancy gold watch in a glass case. While admiring it, the old man casually mentioned that a few of the tribes in the Rockies knew where precious minerals were to be found.

On questioning him, Borke learned of a Crow warrior who always carried nuggets in a pouch, of a Flathead who had told McNair about a great vein of yellow rock far back in the mountains, and about an Ute who had shown the old-timer rough diamonds the Ute found lying right on the ground on a hillside covered with them.

The seed was planted. Night after night Borke tossed and turned, unable to sleep. A hunger gripped him, a hunger that had nothing to do with sickness. He pondered and plotted, and based on information he had gleaned from scores of frontiersmen, he came up with a plan to make himself rich. A deviously simple plan.

What if he were to start up a trading post in the Rockies? He'd already had a lot of merchandise on hand, so it wouldn't set him back financially to pack up some of his goods and transport them across the prairie. Once he had his post up and running, it would be another simple matter to let word get out that he was willing to trade more expensive items, like guns and top-quality knives, for gold and silver and whatnot.

But where to build the post? That had been Borke's main consideration. It couldn't be south of Long's Peak. He'd have too much competition from Bent's Fort. More to the north was better, but not too far north or it would be smack dab in Blackfoot country.

The solution was obvious.

Shoshone territory. By all accounts the Shoshones were the friendliest tribe in the Rockies. They had never taken a white scalp, never so much as raised a finger against a white person. Not only would the Shoshones bring a booming trade in hides and horses, but he could send riders to other tribes with word of what he was really interested in. The news would spread through the Indian grapevine, and before he knew it, Borke would have more gold, silver, and diamonds than he would know what to do with.

That had been the plan, at any rate. So far, it was working fairly well. But Borke hadn't reckoned on Touch the Clouds raising such a fuss about firewater, nor on that other Shoshone, the one who always looked at him as if he were vermin. What was that bastard's name again? He had asked Drags the Rope right before they left.

After a few moments Borke remembered. Hungry Wolf. Something had to be done about him or he would make more trouble. For that matter, if Touch the Clouds didn't stop getting all hot under the shirt every time a young buck got drunk, something might need to be done about him, too.

Artemis Borke hankered to get rich. As rich as King Midas. And he would be damned if he would let anyone, particularly a couple of rotten red savages, stand in his way.

Chapter Five

Her husband was burning up alive and there was nothing she could do about it.

Winona King had never felt so helpless. She had tried everything she could think of and nothing helped.

That first awful day, Winona had stripped off his tattered buckskins and cleaned his many wounds. She had taken her sewing kit from a cupboard and sewn up his scalp and the deeper cuts using a needle made from buffalo bone and thread made from buffalo sinew. She applied herbal treatments and bandaged him.

Among the medicines Winona used were elderberry roots, which had been boiled and mixed into a poultice effective in reducing inflammation. To help combat Nate's high fever, Winona prepared a tea made from the white bark of a plant the Shoshones called *tum kik kola*.

And for a while Winona thought she had succeeded. Nate's fever dropped and his wounds did not show sign of advanced infection. But on the morning of the third day his fever dramatically worsened. His entire body became literally hot to the touch. Worse, his terrible shoulder wound became discolored around the edges, as did several of the deeper gashes on his chest and thighs.

Winona changed his bandages often. She tried *toza*, another tea, concocted from roots of a different plant and widely praised by not only her people but many other mountain tribes as a potent purifier of tainted blood. She spent hours making enough *matoa koa ksi* to apply to every cut and claw mark on Nate's body. It was supposed to help against infection and swelling, and to a degree it did. The discoloration began to clear up, but his fever raged unabated.

Not once did Winona leave her mate's side. She dragged her rocking chair from its usual position near their stone hearth and placed it beside their bed, and there she stayed, day and night, except when she was fetching herbs or making more medicine.

Evelyn tried to get her mother to eat, but Winona only took a few nibbles and gave the food back. Most of the time, Evelyn sat off in a corner, too sad to speak, too depressed to do anything except stare anxiously at her father or woodenly at the floor.

By the fourth day, Winona was on the verge of collapse. She hadn't had more than ten hours' sleep since the nightmare began. Her eyelids weighed tons and her body felt drained and sluggish. For the umpteenth time since sunrise that morning, she placed a hand on Nate's brow and frowned.

"Is he still bad off, Ma?"

"There is no change," Winona said.

"I don't understand. Why aren't any of your remedies working?"

Winona tenderly placed her hand on Nate's bare chest. "The infection has taken root deep in his body."

David Thompson

"What causes it? Did he get dirt into his wounds?"

"The bite of a meat-eater is enough in itself. Remember that grizzly your father shot several winters ago? And the foul odor from its mouth? Bits of meat get stuck between their teeth and rot. Your father told me that creates what the whites call germs. Tiny things we cannot see but which make people very sick."

"I recollect Pa reading about them."

Winona glanced toward her husband's handmade bookshelf, which stood over against the far wall. His prized collection of books crammed the five shelves from top to bottom. Nate had spent years accumulating them, sometimes at considerable expense. They ran the gamut of fiction, geography, history, and more, including a volume on English she had learned by rote—prompting her husband to often joke that she knew his tongue better than he did.

"There must be something we can do," Evelyn said.

Rising, Winona stiffly moved toward the counter, and a large bucket. "We will heat more water and clean his wounds again. I will go to the lake."

"Let me." Evelyn scooted past and scooped up the handle. "I'll be back in two shakes of a fawn's tail."

"I would rather you stay and watch over your father."

"Why? Are you afraid a critter will get me like the bear got Pa?" Evelyn touched Winona's hand. "Don't fret, Ma. I'll take my rifle, and if I run into trouble you'll hear me shoot and can come on the run."

Winona opened her mouth to object but on second thought closed it again. Her daughter was a big girl now. When she had been Blue Flower's age, she had frequently gone off alone into the woods to gather roots and berries. "Very well. But I want you to take a pistol along, as well."

A groan drew Winona's attention to the bed. Nate's lips were moving, but no words came out. He had been fading in and out of consciousness since they brought him back. Usually, adrift in a fever-induced delirium, he jabbered nonsense. But once, for a few minutes the night before, he had been lucid, and had gently squeezed her fingers and told her how much he loved her.

The remembrance brought a lump to Winona's throat. She could not bear the idea of losing him. He was as essentially a part of her as life itself. Never once had she regretted becoming his wife.

Marrying a white man had been a bold step. It had never been done before, and some of Winona's people had been offended. Some *still* were. People like Hungry Wolf and Wallowing Bull, who despised whites due to the color of their skin. To their way of thinking, she had betrayed her people and perverted her heritage.

Winona knew they talked about her behind her back, but she didn't care. Had she to do it all over again, she would still give her heart to Nate. The day they met, that first time she set eyes on him, she had experienced a sensation unlike any other, a feeling that here was the man she was born to be with. Their many winters together had served only to strengthen her love and cement their bond.

Nate was quiet now, his face horribly pale, his breathing labored. Winona caressed his cheek, then turned to tell Blue Flower to be careful. But her daughter was gone. Winona stepped to the door and opened it in time to see her daughter vanish down the trail. "Keep your eyes skinned!" she hollered. "And whatever you do, don't dawdle!"

Suppressing a yawn, Winona stepped outside to breathe deep of the mountain air. It had been so long since she'd left the cabin, she had to squint against the glare of the sun. A robin warbled in a tree to the north. Out on the lake, ducks and geese paddled serenely. The world seemed so peaceful. But it was an illusion, an artful deception. For the plain truth was that under the surface of the wilderness lurked the ever-present threat of having one's life extinguished. As her husband's people would say, Nature had a cruel streak a mile wide.

David Thompson

Winona had learned early on to view the world as it really was, learned early on that the tranquillity of village life was misleading. Protected by warriors, fed and clothed by her parents, she had been lulled by a false sense of security into believing the whole world was a lot like her village. Reality taught her otherwise when Blackfeet raided her band's encampment and wiped out over a score of men, women, and children. People she had known. People she had cared for. Subsequent encounters with wild beasts had further enlightened her to the "way of the world," as Nate called it.

Yet life had its pleasant moments, too. The exquisite joy of loving another. The miracle of childbirth, the supreme happiness of raising a family. Simply *being* alive, being able to greet each new dawn and to appreciate the splendor of each new sunset. There was so much to be grateful for.

Shaking off another yawn, Winona returned indoors. She could use a little coffee. No, make that a lot. Enough to keep her awake until nightfall. Tonight she would try to get enough sleep to see her through the next several days. Because until Nate's fever broke and the infection was defeated, she wouldn't permit herself to rest.

Winona's musing strayed to her son, Stalking Coyote, and his wife, Louisa, who lived in the next valley to the north. She was sorely tempted to ride to them for help, but it was a good day's ride and she couldn't afford to be away from Nate that long. An alternative was to send Blue Flower, but Winona refused to send her youngest on such a long ride alone.

Time passed. Winona stepped to the door, but there was no sign of her daughter. "Blue Flower!" she called, and was upset when she failed to receive a reply. She glanced at Nate, then at the trail. It would take only a couple of minutes to run to the lake and back again. "Blue Flower? Where are you?"

The birds had fallen silent. All Winona heard was the

breeze rustling nearby trees. She took several strides and tried again. "Blue Flower? Answer me!"

Fear welled up. Winona took several more swift strides and was about to bolt down the trail, when she came to her senses. Whirling, she raced inside, armed herself with her Hawken and two pistols, and was retracing her steps to the doorway when she heard a sound that chilled her to her core.

It was a high-pitched cry of alarm.

Every member of Touch the Clouds's band gathered to witness the punishment being administered. Touch the Clouds stood with his great arms at his sides, flanked by Drags the Rope and old Cut Hair.

The Logs went about their business methodically. Ten warrior members of the society ringed Runs Across the River's lodge, and Hairy Man, Log leader, shouted for the offender and his family to come out.

The flap parted. Out strode the young offender. Runs Across the River was armed with a knife and bow, and had the audacity to have an arrow notched to the string. In a rank display of unmitigated arrogance, he yelled, "Go away! I do not acknowledge your right to do this."

Hairy Man was as stocky and powerfully built as he was hairy. Kneeing his mount closer, he asked with the utmost calm, "Is there no end to your transgressions? You have dishonored our people. You have dishonored yourself. Now you must be disciplined. Do not bring more hardship on your family by resisting."

"I have done nothing wrong," Runs Across the River stubbornly insisted.

"You stole firewater from the whites."

"They lie! I did no such thing. I paid for my firewater with the metal disks they gave me for my horses."

"So you claim. Whether you speak with a straight tongue matters little. You have abused your wife's trust. You have behaved in a manner unfitting for a warrior. It is my duty, as head of the Logs, to tell you that you will be made an example of for those who, like you, are too fond of fire-water." Hairy Man nodded at the flap. "Have your wife and children come out, and warn them not to interfere."

Little Grasshopper emerged without being told, one little girl in her arms, the other holding her hand. Chin high, she marched past the waiting Logs.

Hairy Man raised an arm and yipped. At his signal, the Logs closed on the lodge. Some chopped at it with knives, others poked holes with their long lances, effectively hacking the hide to bits and pieces. When it hung in strips, Hairy Man produced a coiled grass rope and tied an end to the bottom of a stout outer lodgepole. A poke of his heels, and his horse slowly backed away. The rope grew taut. Hairy Man jerked and tugged, and momentarily there was a crack and the pole was pulled loose from the rest. He dragged it clear and dismounted to untie the his rope.

"They go about this too slowly," Hungry Wolf griped. "Were I a Log, I would burn it down."

A lot of the bluster had drained from Runs Across the River. He cast a despairing, pleading look at his fellow Shoshones. A few showed some small degree of sympathy, but for the most part their faces were masks of condemnation.

It was too serious a business to be taken lightly. Consequently, no one whooped or yelled when Hairy Man brought the rest of the poles crashing to earth, nor when Hairy Man and four Logs dashed in among the family's personal effects and commenced to break them or cut them up. A doll belonging to Runs Across the River's youngest was spared, as was a dress belonging to Little Grasshopper. But the offender's shield was hacked to pieces, his lance snapped in half. Two other Logs climbed down, relieved Runs Across the River of his bow and quiver, and broke both.

Suddenly someone yelled. Through the onlookers trotted

72

Bear's Backbone astride his best warhorse. He had painted his face and torso and was fitted for war. Wagging a long lance, he defiantly cried, "You will not humiliate me as you have my friend!" Then, reining around, he galloped to the west.

Hairy Man and the Logs accepted the gauntlet. Running to their horses, they gave determined chase, and soon they and their quarry were lost amid the trees.

Runs Across the River shuffled to the site where his lodge had stood and slowly sank to his knees. Fingering a strip of torn hide, he said forlornly, "What have I done? How could I be so stupid?"

Touch the Clouds went over. "Remember this the next time you want to go to the trading post. Firewater brings nothing but trouble."

"I will never visit the whites again!" Runs Across the River passionately exclaimed. "I would rather be gored by a buffalo!"

If only Touch the Clouds could believe him. "If there *is* a next time, I will not be able to prevent the Logs from banishing you." Banishment was the worst punishment the Shoshones meted out. There was no appeal, no reversal. Once the Logs issued their decree, the offender and his family were forcibly escorted into the wild and left to fend for themselves. It was virtual certain death, for few who suffered banishment lasted a winter.

Runs Across the River looked toward his family and shuddered. "If my will proves weak, I beg you to slit my throat and tell my brother to take in my wife and children."

"It will not come to that."

Runs Across the River stood. His lower lip quivering slightly, he responded, "I do not want it to. But I did not want to go back to the trading post again and again for more firewater either, yet I was not able to stop myself. A craving comes over me, a craving I cannot resist."

"Give it no more thought. Go to your wife and girls. They

need to hear you care for them, and you need to hear they care for you."

Hardly had Runs Across the River taken a step when Hungry Wolf and his usual companions blocked the young warrior's way.

"I would have words with you, my friend," the white-hater said. "We offer our sympathy and ask you to join our cause."

Runs Across the River was confused. "What cause would that be?"

"To convince our leaders to drive the whites from our land. Their presence does us more harm than good. You, more than most, have felt the sting of their poison and should be willing to set things right."

"I leave those decisions to our leaders."

"A noble sentiment, but misguided. If a bear were running amok among our lodges, would you wait for our leaders to decide whether to drive it off? You would not. Nor should we sit idle while the whites trick us into drinking their firewater and make us dependent on their trade goods."

Runs Across the River faced Touch the Clouds. "What do you say? I see now you have always had my welfare at heart, and I respect your opinion. Do you favor driving the whites off?"

"Until I have proof they intend us harm, I will not speak against them."

"Waugh!" Hungry Wolf spat in disgust. "Being honorable with men who have no honor is a dishonor to us all. I will never rest in my campaign to persuade our people to do what is best whether they agree or not." Agitated, he slammed his right fist into his left palm. "I would rather give up my spirit than live the lie that the whites are our friends."

"I commend your devotion but question your judgment," Touch the Clouds said. "You talk about honor. But where is the honor in hating those who are different from you for no other reason than they are different?"

Hungry Wolf had more to say, but they were destined never to find out what it was. For as he went to speak, there was a loud *thwack* and he stumbled back, a hole blossoming in the center of his forehead. At the same instant, the rear of his cranium showered outward in a spray of brains, bone, and blood. His friends, spattered with scarlet drops and gory smears of flesh and hair, recoiled in horror and shock.

The sound of the shot came a heartbeat after the slug's impact. Touch the Clouds spun, seeking the source, and spied a spidery puff of grayish-white gun smoke in heavy growth a league to the east. "There!" he cried, pointing, and bolted for his horse. As he pivoted a leaden bee buzzed past, and a woman beyond him cupped her hands to her bosom, uttered a plaintive wail, and fell.

Screams broke out, mixed with bellows of rage. Mothers grabbed children and dashed for their lodges while men rushed to arm themselves.

Again the hidden rifleman fired. *Or is there more than one?* Touch the Clouds wondered. No one could reload that fast. He saw a warrior named Yellow Badger buckle and sprawl in a heap.

The sorrel was staked near his lodge. In no time Touch the Clouds had snatched his bow and quiver from inside his lodge and swung on.

Several other warriors were already riding hard toward the forest. Touch the Clouds swept toward the spot where he had seen the gun smoke, slinging his quiver as he rode. He guided the sorrel by his legs alone, an ability he had mastered when he was still a boy. Yanking out an arrow, he nocked it and drew the string back to his ear. More shots boomed as he covered the intervening ground.

Wallowing Bull was almost to the trees. "I see them!" he exclaimed, one arm hoisted to hurl a lance. "There are two—" A rifle cracked, and Wallowing Bull catapulted off the rump of his animal and spilled to the earth.

Moments later, Touch the Clouds saw them too. A pair of Crows, both with rifles, both swiftly backpedaling toward waiting horses while reloading as fast as their fingers could fly. He centered his shaft on the chest of the Crow on the left and, the instant he was within range, let fly. As always, his aim was true.

The Crow rocked onto his heels. Stupefied, he gaped at the feathered shaft protruding from his body, then reached out to his friend in mute appeal. But the other Crow was taking aim and hadn't seen. Taking aim, in fact, at the nearest Shoshone.

Who just happened to be Touch the Clouds. Whipping out a second shaft, he notched it on the fly. The muzzle of the Crow's rifle centered on him, but he didn't stop, didn't slow down. At a full gallop, he charged, and as he charged he gave voice to a lusty war whoop. His size made him an excellent target, but he also knew it worked in his favor in that it tended to intimidate and frighten his enemies.

The second Crow stroked his trigger.

Flame and smoke leapt toward Touch the Clouds. He felt a tug on his left sleeve, but it wasn't sufficient to spoil his aim. His arrow pierced the man's right thigh, as he intended, and dropped the Crow on the spot. He wanted the second one alive so they could question him. To that end, he balled his huge fist. The Crow was attempting to stand back up. Like an avenging fury, Touch the Clouds bore down and him and clubbed him across the head. And just like that, the clash was over.

Reining up, Touch the Clouds sprang off the sorrel and dashed to the still figures. The first man was dead. As he bent over the second, other Shoshones arrived. A lance was thrust at the second Crow's neck, but Touch the Clouds swatted it aside. "Do not harm this one!"

"Why not?" Elk in Rut demanded.

"We must learn why they attacked us," Touch the Clouds

said, hauling the second Crow up off the ground.

"They are our enemies. They want us dead," Elk in Rut responded. "What more reason do you need?"

There had to be more to it than that, Touch the Clouds reflected. For two lone Crows to attack an entire village was madness. But what if they weren't the only two? What if this had been a diversion of some sort?

Drags the Rope came through the trees and halted. "One is still alive? Do you want me to take him back?"

"I want you to see to it all the women and children are in their lodges. Send warriors to help guard the horse herds and organize a search for more Crows. These two might be part of a larger war party."

The threat of an attack on their village precipitated a mad rush back. Touch the Clouds was left alone. He draped the unconscious Crow across his sorrel, and he was about to climb on when he noticed the Crow's rifle lying in the grass. It was a Hawken, exactly like the one given to him by Artemis Borke. One of the best rifles available, and far too expensive for most Indians to afford. He retrieved the dead Crow's rifle and discovered that it was identical.

Slinging his bow across his back, Touch the Clouds took the guns with him. The initial panic had subsided, and Drags the Rope and Cut Hair had the situation under control. Practically all the women and children were now safely inside their dwellings, and groups of from ten to twenty warriors were fanning out to scour the countryside.

This wasn't the first time the Crows had attacked them. Four times within the past six moons the Shoshones and the Crows had skirmished, with loss of life on both sides. The two tribes had never been on the friendliest of terms, and periodically violence flared, followed by periods of relative peace.

The latest bloodshed stemmed from a dispute over a dead mountain buffalo, of all things. A Shoshone hunting party had spotted it on the crest of a low hill and stalked close enough to kill it. Little did they realize that while they snuck up one side of the hill, a Crow hunting party was sneaking up the other side. Both parties sent arrows into it, and when the bull fell, both claimed it as theirs. In sign language they argued over who had the better claim, and when they couldn't agree, the dispute ended in violence. A Shoshone and a pair of Crows died.

Touch the Clouds had been disappointed by the news. He, along with Nate King, had worked diligently to maintain peaceful relations between the two peoples. Yet here they were, at each other's throats again, each attack inviting retaliation in an ever-escalating series of raids and counter-raids.

It had always been thus, and not just with the Crows. The Shoshones were at constant war with the Dakotas, and had long been at odds with the Blackfoot Confederacy. They had fought the Cheyenne, the Arapahos, and the Utes. Nate King once jokingly asked if there was any tribe the Shoshones *hadn't* tangled with.

A groan ended Touch the Clouds's reverie. He was near the middle of the initial circle of lodges, as good a place as any for what needed to be done. Sliding his right hand under the reviving Crow's shoulder, he unceremoniously dumped the man on the ground.

Crying out, the Crow sat up and clutched at the arrow in his thigh. He gazed around him in growing dismay and recoiled as Touch the Clouds and other warriors surrounded him.

"Do you speak our tongue?" Touch the Clouds inquired. Few Crows did. Sign language was the preferred means of communication. So when the wounded warrior merely sat there, Touch the Clouds held his right hand at shoulder height, palm out, his fingers and thumb extended, and twisted his hand slightly several times. It was sign talk for "question?" He pointed at the Crow, then held up his right hand with his fingers curled and his index finger touching his thumb. Snapping his index finger straight out, he jabbed it at the Crow. It was sign language for "what are you called?"

The Crow glared.

In sign, Touch the Clouds asked why the Crows had attacked. Again the warrior refused to answer. Touch the Clouds asked where the Crows had obtained their new Hawkens, but the warrior wouldn't say. Touch the Clouds informed him that unless he was forthcoming, he would suffer.

"Let us get this over with," urged Buffalo Hump, another close friend of the slain Hungry Wolf's.

Trying one last time, Touch the Clouds offered to spare the Crow if he would cooperate. The Crow sneered his contempt.

Sighing, Touch the Clouds drew his long-bladed knife and stepped closer. Some people were too stupid for their own good. Now they had to do it the hard way. His blade glittering in the sun, he set himself to the grisly task.

Chapter Six

Winona King's heart was in her throat as she sped down the narrow trail toward the lake. Her beloved husband was at death's door, as the whites would say, and now her daughter was in dire danger. She cocked her rifle on the run, crying out, "Blue Flower! Blue Flower! What is wrong?"

The shore spread out before her and Winona lurched to a halt. She had anticipated finding her child beset by another bear or a mountain lion, but instead she saw Blue Flower on her belly, the bucket upended in front of her. "What happened?" Winona asked, dashing to help.

"I tripped, Ma," Evelyn said, her tone one of self-reproach. "Over my own blamed feet! And spilled all the water."

"That is all?"

"What did you expect? I told you I'd fire a shot if something came after me." Standing, Evelyn swiped at splotches

80

of dirt smearing her dress. "Look at me. I'm a mess. Now I'll have to wash it."

Relief washed through Winona, and on its heels came laughter. Hearty laughter that gushed up out of her much as scalding water would gush from a geyser. Once it started, she couldn't stop. Doubling over, she gave vent to a fit of uncontrolled mirth that went on and on and on. She laughed so hard her stomach hurt. Tears blurred her vision, and she sank onto her knees and pressed her sleeve to her eyes to clear them.

Evelyn was studying her as if she had gone crazy. "Are you all right, Ma? I never saw you laugh like that before."

Winona tried to say she was fine, but more mirth spilled out. Maybe it was the result of her emotions being pent up for so long. Maybe lack of sleep was to blame. Whatever the cause, it was a good long while before she could stop. Sucking in deep breaths, she struggled to her feet, feeling as fatigued as if she had run a mile.

"I'm starting to get worried about you," Evelyn said apprehensively. "You haven't been eating enough and you hardly get any sleep. How about if I stay up with Pa tonight so you can catch up on your rest?"

"I can manage," Winona assured her, and affectionately ruffled her daughter's hair. "Right now help me carry this water to the cabin so we can brew tea."

They filled the bucket to the brim and started up. Winona was trying to remember where she had placed a certain small wooden box in which she kept various dried roots, when her daughter asked the last question Winona ever expected to hear.

"Ma, if Pa dies, will you marry again?"

"Your father will not die."

"But if he did, what would you do? Go live with the Shoshones? Find yourself a warrior to sew and cook for?"

Winona had never given the matter any thought. Talking

81

about it troubled her immensely. "Since it will never happen, what does it matter?"

"But if it *did*," Evelyn persisted. "As much as you love Pa, I can't see you marrying again. But I could be wrong."

"I love your father more than I can put into words. I love him with all my heart and all my spirit, and I would sooner die than lose him. He makes me whole."

"How's he do that? You don't have any parts missing."

"Not on the outside. But on the inside we all do. No woman is all she should be. Some have terrible tempers and need a man who can keep them calm. Some are never able to make up their minds and need a man who can help them make decisions. Some are shy and need a man to pull them out of their shells. I could go on and on, but you see my point. And it works both ways. Women complete men as much as men complete women."

Evelyn mulled the revelation until they were halfway up the trail. "I never thought of marriage like that. How does a lady know when a man is the right one to complete her?"

Winona smiled. "Believe me, you will know. Your heart will sing. You will feel as if you are walking on air. You will not be able to eat. And you cannot stop thinking about him. When the two of you are apart there will be an ache in your chest, and when you are together you will feel more content than you ever thought you could."

"It seems like a lot to go through."

"They call it 'love,' daughter, a treasure worth any price. You do not understand, and that is as it should be. No woman truly does until she experiences love for herself."

"I'm in no rush, Ma. If I never find the right fella, it'll be fine by me. Boys are too strange. I could never live with one."

"I thought the same at your age."

The cabin came into sight and Winona walked faster. She disliked leaving Nate alone so long. She had to stay at his side in case he took a turn for the worse. "I'll take the bucket in. Would you be so kind as to gather some extra firewood?"

"Sure thing, Ma."

Winona was setting the bucket on the counter when she saw her husband crumpled on the floor near their bed. Fear knotting her stomach, she reached him in the blink of an eye and hunkered to roll him over. His body still burned to the touch, and when she cracked open an eyelid, his eye was dilated and dull. "Oh, Nate. My sweet, sweet Nate." Had he somehow rolled off? Or had he revived and tried to stand? Winona attempted to lift him but was once again confronted by the daunting challenge of his formidable weight. She tried to work him up over her shoulders as she had when she carried him across the threshold, but he slipped off.

"Need some help, Ma?" Evelyn had returned unheard, carrying an armload of broken branches.

"Yes. Please."

"How did Pa get on the floor?"

"I have no idea." Winona sought to lever her body under Nate's, careful not to jostle his bandaged shoulder, but couldn't quite raise him high enough.

"Hold on," Evelyn said. Depositing the firewood, she darted over. "We did this once before, and we can do it again."

You would think so. But they tried twice to lift him and got him only halfway up, when he would start to slip off and they had to lower him before he fell.

"I do not understand," Winona said.

"Could it be because you're so wore out, Ma?" Evelyn asked. "You must be weak from no food and sleep."

"Could be." Winona wearily stood and contemplated how best to get her man back in that bed. Running a hand through her long black tresses, she had to admit she was stumped.

"Did you hear something?" Evelyn suddenly whispered.

"Hear what, daughter?"

As if in answer, outside their cabin hooves drummed. Winona stiffened. Were they friends or foes? She wasn't expecting visitors. She started toward her rifle, but she hadn't quite reached it when a gun blasted and a wild whoop rent the air.

Crows were courageous warriors. Not fierce, like the Blackfeet. Or devious, like the Dakotas. But very courageous. Crows were also stubborn, and when face-to-face with an enemy, more than a little arrogant. It rendered them bold in battle but brought the most severe torture down on their heads when they were captured, because they invariably refused to cooperate with their captors.

The Crow glaring at Touch the Clouds was typical of his kind. Chin jutting defiantly, he pushed his body back when Touch the Clouds reached for his foot.

"Hold him," Touch the Clouds directed.

Buffalo Hump and Runs Behind each seized an arm. Try as the Crow might, he couldn't break their grip, and he heaped invective on them in the Crow tongue.

Again Touch the Clouds reached for the man's foot. This time the Crow kicked at his hand, and when Touch the Clouds jerked it aside, the Crow surged upward and kicked at his neck. Typical Crow indeed. "Hold his legs as well."

Three men leaped to do so. The Crow resisted fiercely, kicking at each and every one of them, but in due course he was flat on his back, Shoshones firmly holding him by each limb, the arrow still jutting from his right thigh. Blood stained his leggings.

Touch the Clouds removed the Crow's moccasins. Both feet were callused, evidence that the Crow often went without footwear, as did a lot of Shoshones, during the warmer moons. Holding the knife low, Touch the Clouds bent down. The Crow had a good idea what was about to occur, and he violently twisted back and forth in a vain attempt to delay it.

Placing a knee on the Crow's left instep, Touch the Clouds pinned the foot to the ground. He gripped the big toe to keep the Crow from wriggling it, and methodically began to cut the toe off.

A gargled snarl was torn from the Crow's throat. Heaving upward, he made a supreme effort to break free but realized it was hopeless. He grit his teeth against the pain and hissed and sputtered like a rattler that had been trod on.

A moist, sticky sensation spread across Touch the Clouds's hand. He sliced down to the bone, and when he reached it, sawed the knife back and forth. It took a while before the knife sawed all the way through. Holding the toe for the Crow to see, he placed it on the grass, then wiped his hands on the Crow's buckskins. "Are you ready to talk now?" he asked in sign. "Nod if you are."

The Crow stared balefully, radiating an animal lust for vengeance.

Touch the Clouds bent over the foot again. One by one he cut off the rest of the toes and aligned them beside the big one. Blood seeped from the stumps as he worked, forming a puddle under the man's leg.

Every warrior not involved in the search had gathered to watch, and quite a few of the women besides. Some brought their children.

Touch the Clouds cleaned his hands again and signed, in effect, "Why did you and your friend attack us? Are there more Crows nearby?" He didn't expect an answer, and the Crow didn't disappoint him. So he pinned the other foot. This time, instead of cutting off the toes one by one, he elevated the bloody blade above his head, tensed his enormous arm, and arced the knife in a powerful stroke that cleanly lopped all five off in one fell swoop.

Stiffening, the Crow uttered a strangled howl. He tossed his head from side to side, his lips drawn back, his entire face as scarlet as the blood pumping from the stumps of his toes. Huffing like a bull buffalo, he sought to surge up off the ground, but the Shoshones holding him were much too strong. He failed and sank back, limp and whimpering like a kicked puppy.

"Question," Touch the Clouds signed. "Where did you get your rifle?"

Their captive clenched his jaw muscles in spite.

From behind Touch the Clouds, Drags the Rope said, "He will never tell you what you want to know. He would rather die first."

Buffalo Hump agreed, adding, "Why go to all this trouble? Do what has to be done so we can tend to our dead."

"There are mysteries here," Touch the Clouds said. Mysteries he would like to solve. Were it up to him, he would keep the Crow alive as long as possible.

But at that juncture an old woman stepped from among the onlookers, waist-length gray hair framing her wrinkled face in thick braids. "Shall I call them?" she asked, her ancient eyes glittering with relish. "It is the custom," she stressed, as if afraid they would be denied permission.

Touch the Clouds ran his blade across the Crow's shirt to remove the blood, then slid the knife into its sheath and stood. All eyes were on him, the women aglow with anticipation. "Assemble them, Raven's Wing," he said.

With agility belying her years, the old woman spun and sped off to spread the word.

"I am glad I am not this Crow," Runs Behind commented.

Out of the trees trotted Shoulder Blade and Six Feathers at the head of forty more warriors. They had information to impart to Touch the Clouds. Welcome information in one respect, yet disturbing in another.

"There is no sign of a Crow raiding party anywhere in the vicinity of our village," Shoulder Blade reported. "It appears the two Crows were alone."

"Crows have no brains!" Buffalo Hump declared, and some of the younger men grunted their agreement.

"Crows are not stupid," Touch the Clouds said quietly.

Buffalo Hump missed the point. "They are if they send two warriors against an entire village. The Blackfeet and the Dakotas would never be so foolish. They have more respect for our fighting ability."

Shoulder Blade, a man of forty winters whose right shoulder blade had been kicked by a horse when he was five, giving him a perpetual stoop, glanced at the two dozen women who had gathered nearby. "I will rejoin the hunt. I would rather search than watch the Crow meet his end."

"Can it be you have no stomach for it?" Buffalo Hump asked sarcastically.

Shoulder Blade was not one to be trifled with. "Have a care, young one. I have counted more coup than you and most of your friends combined." He reined his mount around. "But to answer your question, I prefer to face an enemy in combat. What our women are about to do is not warfare. My wife and my oldest daughter will take part, and when they do, they are not my wife and daughter."

"Your words have no sense to them," Buffalo Hump said. "How can such a thing be?"

Shoulder Blade and Six Feathers applied their quirts to their horses, and most of the mounted warriors went with them. Touch the Clouds almost wished he could go too. But as a leader he must stay and observe. To not do so would be a slur the women would never forgive. "You can let go of our captive. He is not going anywhere."

Disquiet was spreading, and the men were happy to comply. Most moved a fair distance away and stood in close knots as more and more women streamed in from all parts of the village.

Drags the Rope stayed at Touch the Clouds's side, but his countenance was that of a man sickened by the horror to come.

"You can join Shoulder Blade and Six Feathers if you want," Touch the Clouds said.

"You are my friend. I will stay." Drags the Rope forced

a grin. "We have been through this before, have we not?"

"Do not remind me."

"I, too, have bad dreams for many sleeps afterward. Not of the prisoners, but of what is done to them."

"If you or I were captured by the Dakotas, their women would do the same to us," Touch the Clouds noted.

"Which is why it is better to die in battle than fall into an enemy's hands," Drags the Rope said. "I have often thought that if I were to be wounded and about to be taken prisoner, it would be wiser for me to take my own life than submit."

"Who of us has not had such thoughts? Let us hope neither your nor I ever find ourselves in that position." Touch the Clouds looked at the Crow, who had grown ashen-faced. Their captive's dark eyes were fixed apprehensively on the females, his feet all but forgotten. "I will let you die quickly if you tell me what I want to know," Touch the Clouds signed.

The Crow's hands flowed in reply. "I am not afraid to die."

"I believe you. But this is not a death any warrior would choose."

Tearing his gaze from the swelling ranks of females, the Crow signed, "I know of you, Shoshone. Among my people you are called Mountain-That-Slays. The scalps of many Crows decorate your lodge."

"I never sought trouble with your people. I fight only to protect my own."

"As do I," the Crow signed. "I am called High Hawk. Remember that name. If your people are ever again at peace with mine, tell them how I met my end. It will give my family peace of mind."

"I will do you this favor," Touch the Clouds signed. "Now you do one for me. Why did you and your friend attack us? What purpose did it serve?"

"As I told you, I fight to protect my own."

"Shooting some of us from ambush was pointless. We were not attacking your people."

"But you are planning to," High Hawk signed, and glanced toward where Hungry Wolf still lay. "I heard about that one. He was your war chief. And he planned to lead a raid on the village I am from."

"You are mistaken," Touch the Clouds responded. "I am war chief of the Shoshones, and I have no plan to attack your village or any other Crow village unless your warriors attack a Shoshone village first."

High Hawk's eyebrows pinched together. "You are war chief? How can this be? He gave his word that he spoke with a straight tongue."

"Who did?"

"The one who warned us of your attack. He said he over-heard your war chief talking about it."

"Who?" Touch the Clouds signed emphatically.

At that moment feral yips rose in strident chorus. Scores of women were advancing on the Crow, old Raven's Wing in the lead. Most held knives. Some had tomahawks. A few were armed with lances. One woman wielded a sharp stick.

High Hawk looked longingly to the northwest, in the direction of Crow territory. His throat bobbed and sadness fleetingly rippled across his features. Then he sat up, closed his eyes, and commenced to chant his death song.

Frustrated at not learning the identity of the person who had instigated the attack, Touch the Clouds quickly stepped closer and poked High Hawk to get his attention. High Hawk went on chanting. Touch the Clouds shook him, but the warrior had withdrawn within himself and would not respond.

Raven's Wing gave voice to a trilling cry that brought goose bumps to Touch the Clouds's skin. It was imitated by the pack at her heels. Nearly every woman in the village was now there, and they were terrible to behold. A deeply disturbing change had taken place. Gentle mothers had been transformed into avenging furies. Aged grandmothers had become bloodthirsty specters. Unwed girls, normally so sweet and kindhearted, wore aspects as cold as frigid winter ice.

Touch the Clouds couldn't back away quickly enough. Men were not permitted to take part. This was for the women alone. As it was after a battle, when they roamed the battlefield dispatching enemies who showed the slightest signs of life and mutilating the bodies beyond recognition.

High Hawk chanted louder, but the trilling drowned him out. In solid rows the women ringed him, four to five deep.

A shiver passed through Touch the Clouds, spawned by a blind, fathomless fear as ancient as time itself. He wanted to tear his eyes away, but he couldn't. It wasn't what the women were about to do that affected him so deeply, it was the knowledge that they were *capable* of it. Shoshone women were raised to be brave in the face of danger, and to rally to the defense of their village when it was raided. But this went beyond that. This touched on the fundamental nature of all human beings, and the implications were enough to shrivel the soul of anyone discerning enough to penetrate the truth.

A sharp cry fluttered on the breeze. In somber, silent ranks the women were closing in on the Crow. High Hawk's death chant abruptly ceased, to be replaced by the unmistakable sound of human flesh being hacked and chopped and rent to tiny bits.

"God Almighty!" Orley Harrison bleated, lowering his spyglass. "Do you see what those squaws are doing? *Do you see?*"

Artemis Borke nodded and showed his yellow teeth in a satisfied smirk. "It worked out pretty much as I planned." He tweaked the eyepiece to his own spyglass to increase the clarity. "They shot that uppity buck who wanted to close down our post. But the big cuss, Touch the Clouds, is still alive. That just won't do." They were astride their horses on a hill half a mile to the north of the encampment. Shoshone warriors were scouring the forest below, but none were anywhere near.

Orley raised his spyglass again. "Those heathen bitches! One of them is waving that feller's dingle-dangle in the air!" He shivered from head to toe. "Lord, if they ever get their hands on us . . ."

"They won't," Borke assured him.

"What if that Crow talked? What if he told Touch the Clouds who sold them the rifles? And about the lies we fed him?"

"Relax. The Crows promised they wouldn't tell the Shoshones a thing."

"And you trust a couple of heathens to keep their word?" Orley shook his head. "If you ask me, you take too damn many risks."

"I didn't ask you," Borke snapped. "And the reward is worth it. More money than any of us have ever seen. Gold, silver, maybe diamonds. Enough for all of us to set ourselves up in style, with mansions and carriages and servants to wait on us hand and foot."

"So you keep saying. But I can't live in luxury with my throat slit. If the Shoshones find out the Crows have been sneaking into their territory to pay our trading post a visit, there will be hell to pay."

"How are they going to find out?" Borke demanded. "Are you fixin' to tell 'em? I sure ain't. And the Crows won't, neither, not if they want to go on gettin' guns and trade goods from us."

"I just don't like it," Orley said.

Borke's temper flared and he lowered his spyglass. "No one held a gun to your spine and forced you to come along. I was honest with all of you from the start. I explained the dangers, and I gave you plenty of chances to back out."

"I know. I know. And I'm not faulting you there." Orley's next sentiment was expressed in an appalled whisper. "I just don't want to end up like *him*."

Borke raised his spyglass again. The women had completed their handiwork and were dispersing, their faces glistening with sweat, their expressions strangely empty. There wasn't enough left of High Hawk to fill a whiskey bottle. Not flesh, anyhow. His bones had been stripped clean, as if by a flock of buzzards, and stomped into the dirt. The women had literally flayed him alive. He saw one of them stop and pick something up, a white, pulpy, ropelike object that took him a minute to identify. "A piece of intestine," he breathed.

"What's that?"

"Nothing." Borke would never admit it, but he was every bit as appalled as Harrison.

"Promise me that won't happen, Art," Orley said. "Promise me we won't be chopped up like so much rotten liver."

"I promise," Borke said. But the confidence he felt wasn't quite equal to the confidence he exuded.

Orley nodded at the village. "They're worse than savages. They're monsters. A painter or a bear would never kill like that."

"All the more reason not to have any qualms about fleecin' these red scum for everything we can. They deserve it." Borke spied movement in the woods a few hundred yards off. "We'd best skedaddle before they see us, or that big buck is liable to put two and two together." Reining around, he clucked to his horse.

"What about that big buck?" Orley inquired. "Touch the Clouds is bound to keep buttin' his nose in. How can we be shed of him?"

"I'll have to think on it a spell," Borke said. As his grandpa used to say, where there was a will, there was a way. But savvy was called for. It had to look like an enemy was to blame. The Crows would be reluctant to try after losing two of their own, but there were always the Piegans and the Bloods.

"Maybe Touch the Clouds will do us a favor by falling off his horse and breaking his thick neck," Orley joked.

Artemis Borke grinned. *An accident.* And why not? It would be a lot easier to arrange, and certainly a lot easier to control. Give him a couple of days and he was sure he could think of a means of eliminating the giant without pointing the finger of suspicion at him or his men. "Orley, you're a genius."

"Huh? What did I do?"

"Thanks to you, Touch the Clouds is a goner."

Chapter Seven

Fear brought Winona King to a halt. Fear that a war party was about to attack. Now, of all times. Now, when Nate was helpless and she was so worn out she could scarcely form coherent thoughts.

It could be any one of their avowed enemies outside. The Blackfeet, the Piegans, the Bloods, the Dakotas, Nate had tangled with them all. Not to mention the Arapahos, the Crows, and the Utes. The latter were currently on friendly terms, but the truce was as fragile as a butterfly's wing.

There must be a thousand warriors from a dozen tribes who would give anything to count coup on the mighty Grizzly Killer.

Not if she could help it! Snatching her Hawken, Winona dashed to the doorway. She was fully prepared to sell her life dearly in defense of her loved ones and her home, thereby proving herself a credit to her people and to the wonderful man who had claimed her heart.

Brilliant sunlight stabbed into Winona's eyes and for a few seconds the clearing was bathed in a glow so bright, she couldn't see a thing. Gradually her eyes adjusted enough for her to distinguish the pair of riders who had just reined up. An avalanche of raw emotion overcame her, transforming her to marble and putting a lump the size of an eagle's egg in her throat.

"Great to see you again, Ma," Zachary King happily declared. "Hope you don't mind, but you've got a couple of visitors."

"Stalking Coyote!" Winona breathed in amazement and overwhelming joy, using his Shoshone name as she invariably did with her children. Her oldest was a lot like his father—tall, broad-shouldered, and superbly muscled. His skin, though, was darker, a trait bequeathed by her side of the family, as was his long ink-black hair. Not so the piercing green eyes that gazed so lovingly down on her. They were Nate's eyes. The thought filled her own with tears.

Zach's wife was climbing down. "Is something wrong, Winona?" Louisa asked. A slender young woman with close-cropped sandy hair and wide blue eyes, she wore buckskins that matched Zach's clear down to the decorative beads.

Winona took a step, her arms opening to embrace them. Suddenly she stumbled, dizziness whirling her mind. Her legs became mush. Exhaustion was to blame. Exhaustion from days gone without rest and nourishment, days of unending dread and acute anxiety. They had finally taken a belated toll. Moaning, she pitched forward, and only quick thinking by Lou spared her from striking the ground.

Zach was there in a heartbeat. The two of them tenderly held Winona as she struggled to regain her self-control. She experienced a nigh-overpowering urge to cry, to bawl and bawl until there were no tears left to shed, but she refused to give in. She had her dignity to maintain.

Out of the cabin flew Evelyn, to fling herself like a pint-sized cannonball at her brother. In her zeal she nearly bowled him over. "Zachary! Louisa! Pa's hurt! He's hurt really, really bad!"

Zach's handsome face clouded, and he swept into the cabin carrying her.

Winona attempted to stand, to follow, but her traitor body refused to heed her mental command. She felt so weak, so tired.

"Allow me," Lou said, and helped Winona up. "What's this about Nate?" Supporting her, Lou moved toward the door.

Winona waited until they were inside to explain so her son would hear as well. By then Zach had lifted Nate onto the bed and covered him with a sheet. Louisa eased Winona into a chair; then, at Winona's bidding, hurried to the hearth to finish boiling the water for tea.

"I never thought I'd be glad to see *you*," Evelyn teased Zach from the foot of the bed. "You couldn't have come at a better time."

"Thank Louisa," Zach said, sitting next to Nate. "I was going to wait another week, but she had a hankering to get here sooner." He placed a palm on his father's forehead. "Damn. Pa is hotter than a stove. He's burning up alive."

"Don't you think I know that?" Winona said more defensively than she intended. "I have tried everything I can think of, but nothing will bring his fever down."

"Maybe I should fetch Uncle Shakespeare," Zach suggested. "He knows more remedies than most ten healers combined."

Shakespeare McNair wasn't really an uncle. He was Nate's best friend, and the oldest living mountaineer in the Rockies. He also possessed an intimate understanding of Indian ways. But the mention of "healers" sparked Winona into blurting, "Raven's Wing!"

Evelyn misunderstood. "You want us to go shoot a raven?"

"No, no. Raven's Wing is an old woman from my cousin's band. She is a healer. She knows more about healing the sick and wounded than any other Shoshone. Even more than Shakespeare. If anyone can bring your father's fever under control, she can."

"Then what are we waiting for?" Zach said, rising. "I'll go bring her here."

"But you only just got here," Evelyn impulsively objected.

Like his father, Zach was a man of action. When he made up his mind to do something, he did it, and that was that. He kissed Louisa on the cheek, tenderly squeezed Winona's shoulder, then paused. "If I recollect correctly, Touch the Clouds will be camped on the Green River this time of year. If I push, if I ride my horse into the ground, I can make it there and back in about four days. Can Pa hold out that long?"

Winona patted his hand. "We will make sure he does."

Louisa walked Zach to the door and gave him a parting embrace. "Watch yourself," she cautioned. "There's been talk the Crows are on the prod."

"Can I go along?" Evelyn piped up. "Two people have a better chance of making it there and back."

"Ma needs you more than I would, sprout," Zach answered with a smile. "Make sure she gets enough rest, and give Lou a hand when she asks you." He bestowed a loving gaze on each of them, rotated on the heels of his moccasins, and was gone.

A tiny barb of dismay lanced Winona's bosom. He had stayed so briefly, and now was placing himself in potential peril at their expense. "Come back to us!" she shouted as hooves hammered into the distance.

"Don't you fret too much," Lou said. "That son of yours is as tough as rawhide. Before you know it, he'll be here with the healer."

Winona prayed her daughter-in-law was right. If not, before too long she might be a widow.

David Thompson

* * *

The new day dawned sunny and clear, but a cloud of gloom shrouded the village of the Green River Shoshones.

Touch the Clouds emerged from his lodge to find no one else abroad. The encampment lay as still and quiet as the burial grounds visited the day before when the bodies of the slain were committed to the next world. Relatives of those lost were still in mourning. The wives of the slain warriors had chopped off a finger as a token of their loss, in accordance with Shoshone custom, and would not be out and about for several sleeps. Fathers and brothers had smeared dirt and ash on their faces and chest; mothers and sisters had torn their garments.

The confiscated rifles were now in Touch the Clouds's lodge, along with the rifle given to him by Artemis Borke. When he had placed them beside his, he had been startled to find that all three were exactly identical. He remembered Nate King telling him Hawkens came in different sizes and calibers, and many were custom-made to the specifications of the buyers. How strange, then, that these three should be so alike.

It added to the foreboding that gnawed at Touch the Clouds like a beaver at a tree. He suspected the Crows had obtained their rifles from Artemis Borke. Yet Borke had promised him the trading post was there for the benefit of the Shoshones—and the Shoshones alone. Had the trader lied? And if so, what else had he lied about?

Touch the Clouds began his ritual of greeting Dam Apua, but his heart wasn't in it. The recent events had shattered his usual calm. He had a strong feeling he must act to spare his people more suffering. But act how? Relations with the whites must be treated delicately. Confronting them without definite evidence would antagonize not only Borke's bunch but all white men everywhere.

There was one man who wouldn't take exception, though. One who was white but also Shoshone. A man in a unique position to set things right: Nate King, trapper, mountain man, adopted Shoshone, and husband of Touch the Clouds's pretty cousin, Winona.

Touch the Clouds was proud to call King his friend. When he initially learned that Winona had taken a white man as her mate, lo those many winter ago, he had grave reservations about the wisdom of her choice. The white world and the red world were quite different. Whites were like ants, always scurrying about, always busy, busy, busy, more interested in themselves and the things they owned than the world around them. Shoshones were the opposite. They lived a more relaxed life, stemming in large measure from their philosophy of always striving to live in harmony with the world around them.

Although, now that Touch the Clouds thought about it, maybe the white world and the world of his people were more alike than he was willing to admit. Many warriors, for instance, were preoccupied with how many coup they counted and how many horses they owned. Women gambled for prized colored shells and beads from lands far to the northwest, or were unduly fond of owning only the best hides, the best blankets, the best this or that.

Nate King was more Shoshone than white in that he had no interest in living in a wooden lodge the size of a mountain—or in having servants, as the whites called their slaves, to wait on him hand and foot. Nate had learned to live with Nature on Nature's own terms, as the Shoshones had. To live off the land, as the Shoshones did. And to place more value on people than possessions.

Touch the Clouds came to a decision. He would visit the King lodge and ask Grizzly Killer's help. Nate was a more shrewd judge of white character, and if it turned out Artemis Borke was not the honest trader he claimed to be, Nate could drive Borke from Shoshone territory without arousing the wrath of other whites.

Drags the Rope and Cut Hair must be informed. Touch

the Clouds walked toward his friend's lodge, only to change direction when he spotted Drags the Rope down by the river, standing among a handful of warriors. They were staring into dense woods on the other side, and several had arrows fitted to their bows.

Raiders, Touch the Clouds suspected, and sprinted toward the Green. The Crows would not take the loss of High Hawk and the other warrior lightly. They would require blood for blood, a life for a life. "What is wrong?" he asked as he reached them. Simultaneously, he detected the acrid aroma of smoke.

"Do you smell it?" Drags the Rope said. "Whoever made the fire is unbelievably careless."

Too careless for it to be Crows, Touch the Clouds realized. "Rouse the village. Have half our warriors line up along the bank to repel an attack, and the rest mount their warhorses and await my instructions."

"Wait!" said Shoulder Blade. "Look there! Are my eyes tricking me?"

Riders were threading through the cottonwoods. Three in all, their hats and clothes revealing who they were as surely as if they shouted it from the treetops.

"Whites!" Six Feathers exclaimed in irritation. "They turn up everywhere. Give them ten more winters and they will be as plentiful as rabbits."

Touch the Clouds strode to the river's edge, and the lead rider waved and hailed him good-naturedly.

"Mornin', there, Chief! Me and the boys arrived late last night and waited until now to come on in so as not to spook your braves. Decent of me, wouldn't you say?"

Drags the Rope translated, and Touch the Clouds had him respond, "This is a surprise, Artemis Borke."

"A good one, I trust." The trader drew rein on the opposite bank and leaned on his saddle horn. "Sorry to spring this on you all sudden-like, but I can use your help. That is, if you're still serious about us being pards."

Surprise piled on surprise. "I always speak with a straight tongue," Touch the Clouds confirmed. "What has brought you here?"

Borke's chin bobbed toward the village. "Ain't it customary to invite a visitor in to smoke the pipe of peace before gettin' down to business? Leastwise, that's what a mountaineer I knew once told me."

"You are welcome in my lodge," Touch the Clouds said, and meant it, for it offered him an ideal opportunity to question Borke about the rifles. "Bring your men across. Tell them not to fear. You are under my protection and no harm will befall you."

"I sure as blazes hope not," Borke said, guiding his horse onto a gravel bar. "I'd hate to think I came all this way to do you a courtesy and got rubbed out. I'd be the laughingstock of every coon from here to the Mississippi River."

Touch the Clouds paid particular attention to the trader's tone and inflection, seeking sign of duplicity. Drags the Rope had translated "Mississippi River," a name Touch the Clouds knew as "Great Muddy River," which was what the Shoshones called it. "Those who come in peace are always welcomed in peace," he said.

"It's too bad more folks ain't like you Snakes," Borke commented. "You're the friendliest cusses I've ever met, next to the—" And here he used a word that gave Drags the Rope pause.

"Should we send for Winona King?" Touch the Clouds joked.

Drags the Rope repeated it, rolling the word on his tongue as if it were a type of food he was tasting for the first time. "Qua-kers. Quakers."

"You've never heard of 'em? Quakers live by themselves, on farms, mostly. Sort of their own little tribe, you might say. They believe in livin' by the Good Book and always turnin' the other cheek. You could walk up to one and slap him and he wouldn't lift a finger against you."

David Thompson

"Are there many of these 'Quakers'?" Touch the Clouds had Drags the Rope ask.

"No. They're a drop in the bucket compared to the total amount of white folks," Borke answered. "I met some once, and it tickled me silly how they bent over backwards to please. Me, I believe in what my grandpa always said. Always be friendly, but keep my gun oiled."

Borke's horse climbed out of the river. Next was the man known as Orley, and last a grizzled man who sported tufts of red hair on his chin. "Well, now, Chief. Which tepee is yours?"

Touch the Clouds pointed and strode toward it. Without being bidden, Drags the Rope fell into step. The rest of the warriors brought up the rear.

In their own tongue, Drags the Rope said, "Do you want me to bring Cut Hair and the other elders?"

"We will hear what he has to say first," Touch the Clouds suggested. The more who knew of the visit, the more commotion there would be, and that would attract Buffalo Hump and the other white-haters.

Someone had coached Artemis Borke well. He had his men wait while Touch the Clouds and Drags the Rope went in, and the whites did not enter until Touch the Clouds bid them do so. Once inside, Borke ushered his men to the right and respectfully waited for their host to ask them to sit. Borke was also careful not to walk between the fire and Touch the Clouds. When Orley started to do it, Borke spun and boxed him on the ear. "Didn't I tell you to do as I do, you damned yack? Step between a fire and a Shoshone and they take it the same as havin' a black cat cross your path."

Touch the Clouds's three wives had been busily preparing the morning meal. They were not entirely comfortable with the unexpected arrival of their guests, but they dutifully rose to the occasion and prepared extra food. Their fare consisted of sausages made from buffalo intestines that had been stuffed with marrow and seasoned with wild onions, a boiled pudding made from roots mashed into a flour, and cakes sweetened with berries.

Touch the Clouds rarely partook of coffee, but he always kept a supply on hand for guests. Crooking a finger at his oldest wife, Spotted Wolf Woman, he whispered to her to heat up a pot. Of his three wives, she had been with him the longest. Red Blanket was five winters younger than her, and Chickadee, the youngest of all, had barely seen nineteen winters.

The grizzled white with the red tufts on his chin could not seem to take his eyes off her, a fact both Touch the Clouds and Artemis Borke noticed.

"You've got to forgive my friend, Chief," Borke said with a crooked grin. "He doesn't have the manners of a he-goat." And with that, he backhanded the other man across the face and snapped at him, "Keep those peepers of yours from strayin', Kantner, or I'll carve 'em out of your skull and give 'em to the Snakes as keepsakes."

Borke's display of anger and violence was as rude as Kantner's lechery, but Touch the Clouds let their atrocious lapses pass without comment. It had been his experience that many whites, by Shoshone standards, were rude and callous. Until he met Nate King he had blamed it on differences in their cultures. But Nate had informed him that even by white standards, too many of his own kind had too little regard for the feelings of their fellows.

Artemis Borke placed his hands on his knees and surveyed the interior of the lodge. "Nice place you've got here, big guy. I've never been in a tepee before. There's more room than I'd figured there would be. And I bet it's right cozy on a cold winter's day." He glanced at the vent at the top. "How do they hold up in strong winds?"

Touch the Clouds explained that his people used ten sturdy poles for the framework. Lashed together with rawhide cords, they were anchored to pegs inside the lodge, and arranged so that the lodge tilted slightly. This was done not only so there would be more headroom at the back of the lodge, but also so the longer slant at the front helped brace it against strong winds, which usually came from the west.

"More thought went into these things than I'd reckoned," Borke said by way of an offhanded compliment.

"Great thought goes into everything we do."

"Most people don't go in for houses they can take down and put back up again," Borke said. "They like their buildings to be more permanent. In one country I heard of, a place called Egypt, they've got stone buildings that have been around since before anyone can recollect."

Touch the Clouds made a mental note to ask Nate if that was true. Some white men, and Borke might be one, were prone to exaggerate—or, as the whites phrased it, to tell "tall tales."

Borke wasn't done. "They've got a statue over there, also made of stone, with the body of a painter and the head of a man. No one knows why they made it that way. I met a professor once who tried to convince me it was the statue of a critter that really lived and really looked just like the statue. He also swore there was another critter once, half man, half bull, that was supposed to have run around in some maze somewhere." Borke chuckled. "All that book learnin' must have scrambled the professor's brains."

Touch the Clouds would rather his visitors get to the point of their visit, but he politely refrained from reminding them.

"Strange how different folks can be," Borke philosophized. "My kind is different from yours, and we're both different from those black folks over to Africa, I hear." Borke paused. "Take marriage, for instance. We're only allowed one wife. I never knew you Indians could have as many as you want."

"It is necessary. We lose many warriors in battle, and have many more women than men. So most warriors have two wives or more. But there are a few who take one, and only one, their whole life long."

"You've got three," Borke stated the obvious. "It must make those cold nights even cozier, huh?"

Touch the Clouds wondered if the whites were there to barter for women, to offer trade goods in exchange for companionship. Among some tribes it was condoned, even encouraged, but not among the Shoshones. The only way a white man could share the bed of a Shoshone woman was to take her as his mate.

"I've got to hand it to you, Chief. I couldn't abide being under the same roof with three cantankerous females. All that chatterin' and snippin' would drive me crazy."

"My wives are fine women." The inference that they might not be irritated Touch the Clouds. He chose his wives much as he would choose a new warhorse. Not so much by how they looked as by whether they possessed certain qualities he desired—maturity, tolerance, and a sense of humor. Chickadee, his youngest, was quite mature for the number of winters she had lived.

"I'm sure they are," Borke responded. "But where females are concerned, I'm not like most men. I can take 'em or leave 'em. Some of my boys, though, are as randy as elk in rut."

The trader and his companions laughed at this, but neither Touch the Clouds nor Drags the Rope joined in. "The Crows will let a white man have a woman for the price of a blanket and a knife," Touch the Clouds mentioned.

Borke's jovial mood disappeared and he sat straighter. "Funny you should mention them. They're the reason I've come. I'm here to warn you that a couple of no-account Crows stole some rifles from us. You'd best be on your guard."

Touch the Clouds turned to his wives and asked them to bring over the Hawkens taken from the two dead Crows.

He laid them in front of Artemis Borke and asked, through Drags the Rope, "Are these the rifles?"

The trader picked one up, ran a hand over it, and nodded. "I'll be switched! How did you get hold of 'em?"

"The two Crows attacked us. They rubbed out Hungry Wolf, Wallowing Bull, and others," Touch the Clouds said, watching the three whites closely.

"They attacked your village? Just the two of 'em by their lonesome?" Borke shook his head in amazement. "They weren't too smart, were they? I'm right sorry to hear some of your boys died. It's partly our fault, since our guns were used."

Touch the Clouds could detect no trace of insincerity or deception. "What were Crows doing at your trading post?"

"I didn't invite 'em, if that's what you're gettin' at. They must have stumbled across our post and snuck inside in the middle of the night." Borke uttered a few oaths in the white man's tongue. "I'm just glad it was only the two and not the whole outfit."

"You have seen more Crows?"

"That's the other reason we're here. To ask your help. Those two were part of a Crow war party camped about a day's ride from the trading post. There's twenty to thirty of 'em, too many for me and my boys to tangle with alone. Since it's Snake territory they're invadin', I figured you might like to know."

Drags the Rope stopped translating to say in their own language, "We cannot let a Crow raid go unpunished."

Borke had more to impart. "I took a big chance comin' here, Chief. I should be at the post with the rest of my men in case those thievin' Crows are out to steal all our goods and wipe us out. Will you help? Will you bring your warriors to fight the skulkin' devils? They're still there, last we knew, and don't seem to be in any great hurry to leave. Maybe they're gettin' set to raid your village."

Touch the Clouds could hardly refuse. Shoshone honor

Join the Western Book Club and GET 4 FREE* BOOKS NOW!
A $19.96 VALUE!

Yes! I want to subscribe to the Western Book Club.

Please send me my **4 FREE* BOOKS**. I have enclosed $2.00 for shipping/handling. Each month I'll receive the four newest Leisure Western selections to preview for 10 days. If I decide to keep them, I will pay the Special Members Only discounted price of just $3.36 each, a total of $13.44, plus $2.00 shipping/handling ($19.50 US in Canada). This is a **SAVINGS OF AT LEAST $6.00** off the bookstore price. There is no minimum number of books I must buy, and I may cancel the program at any time. In any case, the **4 FREE* BOOKS** are mine to keep.

*In Canada, add $5.00 shipping/handling per order for the first shipment. For all future shipments to Canada, the cost of membership is $16.25 US, which includes shipping and handling. (All payments must be made in US dollars.)

NAME: _____

ADDRESS: _____

CITY: _____ STATE: _____

COUNTRY: _____ ZIP: _____

TELEPHONE: _____

E-MAIL: _____

SIGNATURE: _____

If under 18, Parent or Guardian must sign. Terms, prices, and conditions subject to change. Subscription subject to acceptance. Dorchester Publishing reserves the right to reject any order or cancel any subscription.

was at stake. The violation of their land and the deaths of their friends and loved ones must be revenged. "I will organize a war party. We will drive the Crows off or slay them."

"I knew we could count on you, highpockets. You're our friend." Artemis Borke grinned at Orley and Kantner. "And you boys were worried about comin' here! I told you we could trust the Snakes. By tomorrow night it'll all work out. Just you wait and see."

Chapter Eight

Zach King owned several horses. His favorite was his dun, a wellspring of energy and stamina he had acquired in trade with a Cheyenne. It could go for hours over the roughest terrain without tiring. Twice in as many years it had saved his life by outrunning hostiles—once when he blundered over a rise onto a war party of Bloods and another time when some Sioux tried to sneak up on him out on the prairie while he was hunting buffalo.

On leaving his parents' cabin, Zach held to a trot until he came to the mountains that rimmed their valley to the north. A long, arduous climb brought him to a pass about nightfall, and once through to the other side, he descended into the next valley at a breakneck pace, aware he was gambling with the dun's life but more afraid of losing the man who meant everything to him.

Zach had always been close to his pa. His ma, too, but it had been his pa he'd spent the most time with once he was old enough to tie his own moccasins. They had done every-thing together—riding, hunting, fishing, exploring. His fondest childhood memories were of the times his pa took him into remote regions of the high country, just the two of them, after game for their larder or just to see what lay over the next mountain range.

Zach hadn't realized it while growing up, but his child-hood had been the kind most boys would give an arm or a leg to have. White boys he had talked to back in the States had mentioned how much they envied him, living way off in the Rockies as he did, and having adventures the likes of which they could only daydream about. Shoshone boys had often told him how lucky he was to be spared the boredom of village life, and to have a father universally acknowledged as a fierce fighter by red men and white alike.

Zach's father once mentioned that childhood was the fur-nace in which a person's character was forged. If that was true, what did it say about his own nature? In many respects he was a chip off the old block, as the whites had it. He loved the wilderness, loved living free, just as his pa did. He cared deeply for the Shoshones and greatly admired their way of life, just as his pa did. But they were different in one crucial respect: His pa thought more highly of white men than he did.

A half-breed's life was a living hell. Many whites and some Indians alike tended to look down their noses at "'breeds," but the whites were worse. Growing up, Zach had suffered, firsthand, the bitter bards of prejudice. He had been treated with contempt for an accident of birth over which he had no control whatsoever.

Some of the incidents were more memorable than others, like the time a trader wrongfully accused him of stealing a knife simply because he was a half-breed, and everyone "knew" half-breeds were "liars, thieves and killers."

Another time, a drunken trapper had tried to take his pony on the grounds it wasn't fitting for a "'breed" to own so fine an animal. His pa had set the trapper straight, but had to knock out four of the man's front teeth in the process.

Small wonder, then, that Zach strongly distrusted most whites. There were exceptions, Shakespeare McNair and Scott Kendall notable among them. But by and large, most whites regarded half-breeds as walking piles of buffalo manure and wanted nothing to do with them.

Which was fine by Zach. Until he met Louisa, he'd wanted little to nothing to do with whites, either. It never ceased to amaze him that after all the hatred he had endured, a white woman had claimed his heart and not a Shoshone maiden or a maiden from some other friendly tribe. Apparently Fate had a sense of humor.

The dun suddenly nickered. Chiding himself for letting his attention wander, Zach scanned the forest. His skin prickled at the sight of spectral forms keeping pace with the dun on either side. Long, grayish, lupine forms, their presence as unexpected as it was unnerving.

Wolves.

Zach automatically lowered his right hand to one of the pistols at his waist, but he didn't unlimber it. Wolves rarely attacked humans. He could count the number of times he had heard about on two hands, and most of those incidents had been in the frigid dead of snow-blanketed winter when their normal prey was scarce and they were half-starved. The animals flanking him were healthy, well-fed specimens in their prime, their coats sleek and thick, their bodies layered with muscle. He doubted they would try to bring the dun down. But then again, his pa had another saying well worth remembering: Never take a predator for granted.

The lead wolf was a big male, loping along on the right, a splendid beast with a luxuriant coat. Zach grinned, and on an impulse let out with a wolfish howl. To his delight, the leader threw back its head and outdid him. That served as a signal for the rest of the pack, which unleashed an undulating chorus that wafted down the mountain and out over the foothills.

Zach laughed in pure glee. The wolves at his side, the wind whipping his hair, the feel of the dun under him, sent an intoxicating zest pumping through his veins. He howled again, and the big wolf echoed him. Zach shifted. For a moment their eyes met, the wolf's glowing palely in the light of the half-moon. Then, as mysteriously as they materialized, the pack was gone. One instant he could see them; the next they melted into the inky night.

Disappointed, Zach raced on. Presently heavier timber rose before him. The moonlight didn't penetrate the forest canopy, forcing him to slow. He had gone perhaps a mile and a half when a sharp crash alerted him he wasn't alone. He had acquired another shadow, only this one wasn't long and gray and lupine. It was huge and brown and ursine, hundreds of pounds of solid sinew and bone sculpted into the most formidable beast in the wild.

A grizzly was shadowing him.

Cold sweat broke out, and Zach almost lashed the dun into a gallop. But fleeing might incite the bear into giving chase, and in the thick woodland, outrunning it was out of the question.

The dun's eyes were wide, its ears pricked, its nostrils dilated. It was, in short, scared to death, and it wouldn't take much to goad it into making a mistake that could cost them both their lives.

Keeping a tight rein, Zach watched the grizzly for some sign of what the brute intended. The monster had a deceptively awkward, lumbering gait. Many a trapper and mountain man had made the mistake of thinking silvertips were as slow as molasses when in reality the only animals fleeter of foot were antelope.

A low *whuff* emanated from the bear's massive chest, and it raised its enormous head to test the wind.

Zach wrapped his hand around a flintlock. The next few

seconds would decide the outcome. Bears were walking stomachs attached to a nose. If this one was hungry, their scent would provoke it into attacking in a flurry of snapping jaws and rending claws. He might get off by a shot, but the odds of hitting a vital organ were slim. A bear's brain was protected by the thickest skull in the animal kingdom, and its heart and lungs by enough tissue, fat, muscle, and hair to absorb the heaviest of slugs.

The grizzly angled nearer. It was only ten feet from the dun, the giant hump between its front shoulders as distinct as the wicked set of rapier teeth visible when it abruptly shattered the night with a ferocious roar.

The brute had made up its mind! Zach reined to the right and slapped his legs against his mount. Whether he survived depended on the dun, and on a heaping portion of pure luck. Behind him, brush and small trees crackled and snapped to the grizzly's headlong passage. It wasn't moving at its top speed yet, but it soon would be.

Exhibiting horsemanship that would fill his father with pride, Zach hauled on the reins again, cutting to the left. The change of direction forced the bear to turn, too, slowing it a trifle. And every yard gained added precious moments to his life span.

Another roar shook the very ground.

Zach reined to the right, between a pair of tightly spaced oaks, and smiled when the grizzly slammed into them like a runaway wagon and was knocked back onto its haunches. He gained more ground. But not enough. Not anywhere near enough.

Head down low, the bear hurtled around the oaks and bore down on the dun like a dislodged ten-ton boulder on a high slope. It plowed straight through a thicket Zach had skirted, regaining the ground it had lost.

Zach twisted around. The hulking behemoth was so close, he swore he could feel its hot, fetid breath fan his neck. Enormous legs powerful enough to rip apart logs were pumping in ponderous cadence. Four-inch claws glinted yellowish. The creature was gigantic, its great hump as high as the horse. Zach was pitted against a colossal engine of destruction, literal savagery incarnate, inviolate in its domain, the lord of all it surveyed.

The bear was now close enough to tear the dun's rump open with a single swipe. But fortunately for Zach and his mount, it couldn't run and slash at the same time. It snapped at the dun's flanks instead, gnashing and rending its array of saber teeth. So far its iron jaws hadn't connected, but it was only a matter of time. Perhaps mere seconds.

Zach faced forward just as a tree hove out of the gloom, a forest patriarch, a white pine that had to be fifty feet high with a trunk three feet wide. A less experienced rider would not have been able to avoid it. But Zach had been taught to ride as soon as he could sit a pony. In addition, a lifetime of perilous wilderness existence had honed his reflexes as sharp as a straight razor. With him, thought and action were nigh instantaneous. The very split instant he saw the obstacle, he reined sharply to the left to avoid it.

The dun missed reaping disaster by the width of a whisker.

The grizzly's reflexes weren't quite as quick. At full speed it slammed into the bole. There was a resounding thud and the entire tree swayed, the impact flinging the griz onto its side.

Zach whooped for joy. He figured the bear had to be crippled or at least dazed. It couldn't possibly catch him now. But he was mistaken. For with a tremendous roar of commingled pain and baffled rage, the monster shot to its feet and took off after him with renewed vigor, showing no ill effects of the collision whatsoever. The bear was, if anything, moving faster than before, its eyes seeming to glow with an inner bestial light all their own. This time there would be no stopping it short of death—its, or his own.

David Thompson

Zach was in for the ride of his life. He flicked his reins and bent low over the pommel. But not low enough. A low branch swept out of nowhere and caught him flush across the chest. Excruciating torment spiked through his body as he was swept out of the saddle and sent tumbling to earth in a whirl of arms and legs. His shoulders bore the brunt. He couldn't tell where he had landed in relation to the griz but feared it was directly in the animal's path. Desperate, he struggled to get his hands under him and stand. Before he could, a black veil enveloped his senses.

The last sound he heard was a terror-struck whinny.

Her husband stopped breathing in the middle of the night.

Winona had fallen asleep in the chair by the bed. She dozed fitfully, in snatches, waking up at the slightest sound or the slightest movement on his part. Often she touched his brow, and whenever she did, the lines in her haggard face deepened. His temperature was as high as ever. Her teas, her herbs—it had all been ineffective. She was losing him, losing the love of her life, losing the noble heart with which hers was entwined, and it tore at her insides like the molten cauldrons in the land of many geysers.

"Please, Nate," Winona whispered, her eyes damp with the overflow of her emotions. "Please do not die on me. I love you too much to lose you."

Dabbing at her tears with a sleeve, Winona got up, moistened a cloth, and placed it on his forehead. The cabin was chilly. Earlier she had opened the window to admit the brisk night air, hoping it would help cool his fevered form. But it, too, had proved unavailing.

Winona glanced toward the corner where Evelyn slept, bundled under a heavy Mackinaw blanket. There was no telling how losing Nate would affect her. But Winona guessed it would intensify Evelyn's dislike of the wilderness and heighten her resolve to move to civilized parts once she was old enough to make do on her own.

Over against the right wall was another bundled blanket, with Louisa's head poking from the top. She had been of great help, and only turned in at Winona's insistence. No one could ask for a better daughter-in-law.

Settling into the chair, Winona closed her eyes. She had to face the terrible truth: Zach wouldn't return in time. Four days was too long. Nate would die before the healer reached them. The burden of saving him was on her shoulders, and her shoulders alone. But she had tried everything her mother and grandmother ever taught her. She couldn't think of a single thing she had overlooked.

Thinking took effort. Her fatigue was chronic, as much a part of her as breathing. She had never been so tired for so long. It was bound to inhibit her mental faculties. She had doubled her coffee intake to combat it, but the coffee no longer helped.

Shifting to relieve a cramp, Winona heard the *crack* of a twig through the open window. Something was out there, something large. Ordinarily she would get up to investigate, but she was too physically spent and mentally sluggish to try. All she did was lift her head, and when the sound wasn't repeated she sank back down.

Winona needed sleep. She was honest enough with herself to admit that unless she caught up on her rest she would be of no use to anyone. Certainly not to Nate, who needed her as he had never needed her before. Slumber eluded her, though, and for restless minutes she tossed and fidgeted, brimming with anxiety she couldn't contain.

Finally Winona's brain refused to function. She was on the verge of total collapse when her frayed mind succumbed.

At the precise second Winona passed out, she happened to be gazing at the window. In the depths of her fatigue, she imagined she saw a face peering in at her—a cold, emotionless face carved from stone.

Then her world faded to black.

David Thompson

*   *   *

Once again a new day dawned, but Touch the Clouds did not greet it the usual manner. He was no longer at the village. At the head of a large war party, he had left the day before and ridden hard toward the trading post. They had not been able to reach it before nightfall, so they made camp on a grassy flat bordering a gurgling stream. The thirty warriors accompanying him were in a somber mood. Painted for war and fully armed, they were determined to drive the Crow invaders from Shoshone territory or die trying.

Artemis Borke and his two friends were in surprisingly fine spirits, given the circumstances. Borke couldn't stop apologizing for letting the Crows steal rifles from under his nose.

The whites made their own camp a short distance from the Shoshones. After posting guards, Touch the Clouds walked over, taking Drags the Rope and Shoulder Blade along. He had the former ask, "Why do you sleep by yourselves? You are welcome to join us."

"That's right hospitable, Chief," Borke responded, "but I've seen how some of your bucks look at me and my pards. They're holdin' a grudge on account of Hungry Wolf and those others the Crows shot. It's best if we stay apart."

Touch the Clouds understood. Some warriors did blame the whites for the deaths, just as the whites were blamed for the shame reaped by Runs Across the River and the banishment of Bear's Backbone.

"I'd like to get in their good graces again," Borke commented. "But short of givin' merchandise away for free, I'm stumped as to how to go about it. What would you suggest?"

"Side with us against the Crows."

Borke leaned back. "In case you ain't noticed, I already have. I came to warn you about the rifles being stolen, didn't I? And I'm willin' to lead you to the Crow camp so you can wipe them out. What more do you want?"

"Fight with us," Touch the Clouds clarified. "When my people see you shed Crow blood, they will accept you as a friend."

"Kill Crows?" Borke looked as if he had swallowed a burning ember. "I'm a trader, hoss, not a soldier. I don't go around makin' war on folks. This business is between your two tribes."

"You asked what you could do," Touch the Clouds said.

Borke pursed his thick lips. "It would land me in a heap of hot water. The Crows will count me as an enemy and try to burn my post to the ground." He shook his head. "I have enough of a hard time keepin' your people from runnin' me off. I don't want to add to my woes."

Orley whispered something. Borke nodded, then said, "How about if I gave five or six rifles to some of your closest friends? Wouldn't that show I was sincere?" He looked at Touch the Clouds and blinked. "Wait a second. Where's the rifle I gave you? Why didn't you bring it along? Don't you like it?"

"The rifle is a fine weapon," Touch the Clouds conceded. But he had fired a rifle only twice in his entire life, and then only after Nate King loaded it for him. Guns felt alien in his hands, and he was so slow at loading and so poor at hitting a target, for him to use a gun in battle would be rank stupidity. With a bow, on the other hand, he was a master. He could unleash a dozen shafts in the time it took a white man to fire a rifle twice, and all twelve would hit their targets dead center.

"It seems to me you'd be happy to have a Hawken," Borke grumbled. "Tribes with guns always beat tribes without guns. It's happened time and again."

Touch the Clouds did not like being reminded. Firearms were upsetting the balance of tribal power to a degree not seen since the advent of the horse. Long ago, most tribes had been evenly armed, and the number of warriors a tribe could muster counted for more than anything else. But the

David Thompson

horse changed that. Tribes with horses could travel farther, strike harder, and escape faster. Soon every tribe had to have them, and once again a balance was struck.

Now came guns. The Blackfeet had appreciated their potential early on and acquired all the guns they could lay their hands on. As a result, the Blackfoot Confederacy had become the most powerful tribal group in the northern mountains and plains. They raided far and wide with impunity, striking into the heart of Cheyenne, Crow, Dakota, and Shoshone country. So the rush was on for other tribes to acquire guns.

Borke sipped some coffee and said, "Play your cards right, hoss, and I'll see to it your people have more guns than they know what to do with. With my help you can become the strongest tribe in these parts. Wouldn't you like that?"

The temptation was appealing. Touch the Clouds had seen too many of his people killed in raids or ambushed from hiding by cold-hearted invaders bent on a ruthless campaign of extermination.

It had always been thus. Since as far back as any Shoshones could remember, back into the dim depths of legend and antiquity, warfare was woven into the skein of Shoshone life. Simply put, there was never a time the Shoshones weren't at war with someone. Their first enemies had been the red-haired cannibals who once dwelled in the western ranges of the Rockies. Holdovers from an earlier era, the cannibals had preyed on humans much as humans prey on deer and elk. Over the course of countless winters the Shoshones had worn their foes down, a war of attrition that ended when a famous chief drove the few remaining cannibals into a cave and sealed it so they could never get out.

Then came conflicts with other tribes. Everyone from the Blackfeet to the Utes to the Dakotas. A constant cycle of attacks and counterattacks, raids and reprisals. War without cease. Bloodshed without end.

As a consequence, the Shoshones became a warrior nation. They adopted many of the practices of the militant plains tribes. They acquired the horse. In an increasingly hostile world, they were able to hold their own.

Nate King once joked that if it hadn't been for waging war, most Indians would sit around twiddling their thumbs. Uttered in jest, his comment contained a kernel of truth. No one knew that better than Touch the Clouds. As war chief of the Shoshones, he was as versed in the history of tribal war as he was in its practice.

Touch the Clouds had never told anyone, but he was sick to his spirit of the continual killing. When he thought of all the loved ones and friends he had lost, when he realized that long after he was gone war would continue to rule Shoshone life, a pall of sadness descended. Surely there had to be more to life than that? Surely the Great Mystery wouldn't be so capriciously cruel?

"Wouldn't you like that?" Artemis Borke repeated when he didn't receive an answer.

"To be the strongest tribe in the mountains?" Touch the Clouds said. "I would settle for being the safest."

"Then you need guns. Other tribes won't dare lift a finger against you if your people have a rifle in every tepee. Think of it! The Snakes would be invincible!"

Touch the Clouds did think of it. Long after he lay down to sleep, he pondered what it would be like if every warrior owned a gun. And the conclusion he came to was that it wouldn't change a thing. Because their enemies would also acquire more guns, and the unending cycle of battle and bloodshed would never end. If anything, it would grow worse. There would be more lives lost on all sides, until eventually every tribe would share the fate of the ancient red-haired cannibals.

Touch the Clouds thought about it some more the next morning over a breakfast of pemmican and water. Before sunrise they were on their warhorses, and by the middle of the morning they were within sight of Dead Elk Creek. They followed its meandering course to the trading post and were warmly greeted by the whites who had stayed.

Artemis Borke conferred with them and excitedly relayed the latest news. "My men say a passel of Crows paraded around the post last night, showin' off. That war party must still be camped where I saw it last. We're in luck."

"How far to their camp?" Touch the Clouds asked.

Borke pointed at a range of jagged peaks to the northwest. "Yonder. We can be there by midafternoon, but I wouldn't push too hard if I were you. We don't want to give ourselves away."

Touch the Clouds was ready to leave immediately, but Borke insisted his men needed to change horses. Touch the Clouds saw no sense to it; their animals were in fine condition. But he did not object. As a result, a lot of time was wasted as Borke, Orley, and Kantner took their mounts into the stable, unsaddled them, and transferred the saddle blankets and saddles to fresh horses.

Soon after, Borke led the Shoshones through the gate. They moved in single file, as quietly as the terrain allowed. What little conversation there was, they conducted in sign language.

Touch the Clouds had been to this stretch of country before. A maze of gorges and erosion-worn ravines made it ideal for a war party to hide in. The extremely rocky ground bore few prints, and enemies could be seen from a great distance from atop any of the many high ridges.

Unhesitatingly, Artemis Borke guided them to the mouth of a narrow defile. Barely wide enough for a horse, it wound deep into the wasteland between walls of solid stone that towered higher than an arrow could reach. Drawing rein, he whispered, "This is the place. Follow this and it will take you right to the Crow camp."

Touch the Clouds scanned the ramparts, wondering why it was the Crows had not posted lookouts.

"You and your braves better go ahead," Borke suggested.

"You have more experience at this sort of thing."

A jab of Touch the Clouds's heels sent his warhorse into the opening. He did not like being hemmed in, but it couldn't be helped. Drags the Rope and the rest of the warriors followed his example. They negotiated a number of turns and were midway along a straight stretch when a shadow flicked across the defile, attended by a crunching noise. Snapping his neck back, Touch the Clouds was stupefied to behold a large boulder roll over the right rim and plummet toward them.

Chapter Nine

The sound of a multitude of birds warbling and chirping in raucous racket penetrated the emptiness in which Zachary King was enveloped. His thinking was hazy, confused, and he couldn't remember where he was or what he had been doing when he fell asleep. Cracking his eyelids, he was amazed to find he was lying on his side on the ground. He started to rise, and a sharp pain speared his chest. It jarred his recollection of the nightmare chase, and the grizzly that by rights should have eaten him.

To the east a golden crown bedecked the world. It was dawn. Zach had been unconscious for hours. Gingerly feeling his ribs, he slowly sat up and took a look around. The bear was nowhere in sight. Nor was the dun.

Their tracks told him why. From where he sat, Zach could clearly see that his horse had kept on going after he was knocked off and the bear had barreled after it, more interested in horseflesh than human flesh.

Zach slowly stood. He felt stiff and sore, but he wasn't seriously hurt. Even better, his pistols were undamaged, and even better yet, neither was his rifle, which lay a few yards away. Brushing dust off it, he debated what to do.

The dun had fled to the north. Touch the Clouds's village was to the northwest. Zach would lose valuable time if he set out after his mount and wind up miles farther from his goal. By the same token, it would take him ten times as long to reach the village on foot as on horseback, so if there was any chance, any chance at all, that the dun was still alive, it made sense for him to go after it.

Cradling his rifle, Zach traveled at a steady, mile-eating jog. Clods of earth churned by the dun's flying hooves and a wide swath of trampled brush left by the massive bruin made tracking them ridiculously simple. He was heartened to see that the dun had stayed ahead of the bear. At least for a time.

A quarter of a mile farther on, Zach came to a steep slope the animals had descended. The grizzly had practically been nipping at the dun's tail. Both lost their footing. Deep furrows marked where the horse slid the last seven or eight yards. As it tried to straighten, the bear overtook it and there had been a struggle. Splotches of dry blood brought an oath to Zach's lips. He was encouraged, though, to find that the dun had made it to its feet and galloped off. Right behind it, however, had been the griz.

The sun cleared the horizon. As Zack jogged on, bright sunshine splashed over the woods, transforming them from a murky realm of shadows and latent menace to a wonderland of pristine beauty and tranquillity. It was an illusion responsible for the deaths of many an unwary soul who let down their guard when they shouldn't.

Zach knew better. When a loud snort sounded to the west, he immediately halted. The undergrowth crackled noisily, growing louder and louder, and soon immense shaggy shapes appeared. Five or six mountain buffalo, distinguished from their plains brethren by their shaggier, darker coats, passed within sixty feet of where he stood and never suspected he was there. It helped that the wind was wafting his scent away from the temperamental beasts. He waited a couple of minutes after the sounds faded to be sure they were gone, then moved on.

By the tracks, the dun had been hard-pressed at that point, and it had woven back and forth in a desperate bid to shake the meat-eater. Another hundred steps, and Zach broke into a broad grin. The bear had given up. It had stopped dead and let the dun go. Stamina triumphed over brute force. For although grizzlies could move with astounding swiftness when they were so inclined, they tired much sooner than a horse would. The bear they had encountered chased the dun a lot farther than most of its kind would, but at last, its endurance sapped, it had been left with nothing to eat but the dun's dust.

From there the griz had wandered eastward while the dun fled on to the north. It hadn't slowed until it covered another half a mile. Occasionally, scarlet drops speckled the vegetation.

Zach was worried that his mount had been grievously hurt and might need to be put down. He had an aversion to killing horses and would do all in his power to save it.

Midmorning arrived, and Zach emerged from the woods into a rolling valley lush with grass. "Parks," the mountain men called them. A small herd of black-tailed does grazed unconcerned nearby, and across the valley, in the shade of encircling trees, lazed a quartet of tall elk. A solitary animal near the middle of the valley interested Zach more. He raced toward it, dreading what he would find.

The dun was caked with dust and matted with dry sweat. Its reins dangling, it was cropping the sweet grass, so hungry that it didn't raise its head at his approach.

"Easy there, fella," Zach said soothingly in order not to spook it. Slowly walking up, he snagged the reins. A few claw marks on its rear legs testified to the close shaves it had had, the worst a wicked gash on its flank. But none were life-threatening.

As careful as could be, Zach mounted and reined to the northwest. To the best of his recollection there was a creek not far off, and the dun's wound needed to be cleaned. "Then it's on to Touch the Clouds's village," he said aloud. He tried not to think of the time he had lost or dwell on the potential consequences.

"I'll save you, Pa," he vowed. "If it's the last thing I do."

The pressure of fingers on her arm dragged Winona King from a deep, dreamless sleep. She waded through a thick mental fog, her exhausted body reluctant to return to the land of the living. Someone urgently whispered her name and shook her, and she sat up in the chair and opened her eyes. Sunlight slanting through the window told her it was shortly past dawn. "I am awake," she announced to stop the shaking. Her first thought was that her husband had taken a turn for the worse. "What is all the fuss?"

"We have visitors, Ma."

Evelyn was by the chair, as rigid as a ramrod and as pale as a sheet. Louisa, over by the table, was also petrified but trying not to show it. The cause of their fright were four swarthy warriors in buckskins who stood just inside the open front door, their features as inscrutable as smooth clay. The style of their buckskins and moccasins, and the fashion in which they wore their braided hair, pegged them as Utes.

Winona shot erect, blurting, "How did they get inside?"

"They were waiting out front," Lou answered. "When I opened the door to go feed the horses, they barged on in."

Terror gripped Winona. At one time the Utes had claimed the valley as theirs, and for years waged a relentless campaign to kill her family or drive them out. Then her husband did the Utes a great favor at the request of an Ute chief, and in return the Ute leader gave his word that their family could go on living there unmolested.

Utes hadn't visited the valley since. For four of them to invade her home did not bode well. Winona sidled toward the wall where her rifles were propped, but the tallest Ute divined her purpose and moved to block her.

"I asked them what they wanted," Lou said, "but they don't speak English or Shoshone."

Winona tried sign language. "Question. What do you want?"

The tall Ute came toward her. He was of middle age, his hair graying at the temples. Not bothering to respond, he gazed over her shoulder at the bed where Nate lay.

"What do you want?" Winona repeated. She regretted placing her pistols on the counter the night before, and considered making a try for them.

Tucking a war club he held under his left arm, the tall Ute signed, "Question. Your man is sick?"

"A black bear mauled him," Winona disclosed.

"I would look," the Ute signed, and without awaiting permission, he strode past her.

Winona grabbed his arm to stop him, then froze when one of the other Utes trained a bow on her and started to draw back the string.

"Watch out, Ma!" Evelyn hollered.

Tugging his arm free, the tall Ute walked to the bed. His brow knitting, he placed a palm on Nate's forehead and said something to his companions in the Ute tongue.

"Do you have any notion what they're saying?" Louisa asked.

Winona shook her head. A knowledge of Ute wasn't included in her linguistic storehouse. "I want you to leave," she signed to the tall one. "My husband needs rest. He must not be disturbed."

The tall Ute shocked her by signing, "We will take him with us."

126

"You will do no such thing!" Winona was at her husband's side in two bounds. Shoving the tall Ute away from the bed, she signed, "Try to hurt him and I will hunt all four of you down and count coup on your bodies."

"We must take him," the tall Ute insisted, and motioned for her to stand back. When she refused, he seized her by the shoulders to move her by force.

Deep inside Winona something snapped. Fury such as she had seldom felt exploded through her. Swatting his hands off, she grabbed for the knife at her hip. The Ute cried out to his friends and pounced. Before she could unsheathe her blade, her wrists were clamped in iron vises and she was shoved against the wall.

Louisa and another Ute began scuffling. Evelyn had made a dash for her rifle but never made it. A third warrior hooked an arm around her waist and held her up off the floor despite her enraged efforts to gouge and kick him.

Winona fought back as savagely as a bobcat protecting her brood. She had no idea what the Utes were up to, but given that her husband had slain more than a few Ute warriors before the truce, she dreaded the worst. For all she knew, they were going to drag him back to their village and torture him. She would give her life before she let that happen.

Shifting on the ball of her foot, Winona arced a knee at the tall Ute's groin, but he blocked the blow with his forearm and retaliated by slamming her against the wall.

Evelyn, meanwhile, had twisted and was clawing at her captor's eyes. She missed and raked his cheek. To stop her from doing it again, he enfolded her in his other arm, pinning both of hers. She could still move her legs, though, and move them she did, but the majority of her kicks glanced off his legs, doing no real harm.

Louisa fared little better. She broke her assailant's grip and heaved up off the floor, only to be tackled from behind by the fourth Ute, a burly warrior who outweighed her by a good hundred and fifty pounds. She was pancaked against the floorboards with the burly Ute straddling her back.

Only Winona was left to resist. Again she clutched at her knife and succeeded in clearing it, but lost her hold the very next moment when it was smashed from her grasp. A callused hand gripped her by the hair and snapped her head back. Eyes as dark as her own bored into hers, and the tall warrior hiked his war club.

Winona still had plenty of fight left. Balling her right fist, she punched the tall warrior flush on the mouth. It caught him off guard; Indians rarely resorted to their fists. She landed a second punch, rocking him on his heels. Taking advantage, she slid her right foot behind his and drove her shoulder against his chest.

The tall Ute stumbled backward. Onto the bed. And onto Nate. Getting a hand under him, he raised his war club.

Winona lunged. Grabbing the warrior's left foot, she pulled with all her might. She only intended to slide him off Nate, but she yanked him clean off the bed, toppling him onto his hands and knees.

Spying her knife by the front bedpost, Winona dived for it, but the tall Ute caught her and flung her against the chair. It went down with her on top. She heard her daughter yell and felt a searing pain above her left ear. The warrior had struck her a glancing blow on the head with his war club. It didn't knock her out, but it did render her incapable of resisting as he drew his knife and cut several long strips from the sheet she had covered Nate with. The Ute used one strip to bind her wrists behind her back. The other strips were used to tie Evelyn and Lou.

"We're goners, Ma," Evelyn said forlornly. "They're fixing to kill Pa, I bet, and keep us prisoners the rest of our born days."

Lou sat up, scowling. "I will never let another man lay a hand on me!" she cried. "Only Zach has that right!"

Winona said nothing. She blamed herself for their plight.

If she had not let herself become so worn down, if she had been more vigilant, if she hadn't drifted off after spying that face in the window—if, if, if. Recriminations were pointless but in this case justified. She had let her loved ones down, and now her mate might pay the ultimate price for her care-lessness.

The Utes were conferring. One rubbed the marks left by Evelyn's nail on his cheek. Another limped slightly. The tall warrior had a bloody lower lip. Abruptly, an argument en-sued. Whatever it was about, the tall warrior seemed to get the best of the dispute, and soon he and another warrior moved to the head of the bed and slid their hands under Nate's shoulders.

Winona racked her brain for a means of stopping them. She was between the upended chair and the bed. She could try to trip them as they went by, but they might drop Nate.

"What do we do, Ma?" Evelyn cried. "What do we do?"

The warrior with the limp poked the tip of his lance into Winona's side. Not deep enough to draw blood, but hard enough to convince her to stand when he gestured for her to do so.

To Winona's dismay, the sheet covering Nate slid off. She had removed his clothes in a bid to cool his fevered body, and now he was exposed to her daughter and daughter-in-law. It was most unseemly. Shoshones were reserved where their bodies were concerned, and public nudity was frowned on. Even when couples made love, they did so par-tially clothed or with a blanket over them.

The tall Ute noticed her reaction and halted. He reached for the sheet, then spotted Nate's buckskin pants neatly folded on top of the chest of drawers. Unfolding them, he crouched and slid Nate's feet into one leg and then the other.

"Why did he go to the bother of doing that if all they aim to do is kill Pa?" Evelyn wondered.

Winona didn't know, and the uncertainty compounded

her fears. The warrior holding the spear jabbed her again, indicating she should follow the pair bearing Nate. She was all too happy to accommodate them, as she had no intention of letting her husband out of her sight. Evelyn and Lou came behind her. Last was the fourth Ute, his bow elevated for quick use.

Four mounts waited at the tree line, but the Utes bent their steps toward the trail to the lake instead.

"What are these coyotes up to?" Lou said. "I thought they would take us to their village. I don't like this, not one bit." Stopping, she set herself. "And I'll be damned if I'm taking another step."

The fourth Ute had other ideas. Using the flat of his hand, he propelled her forward and wagged his bow to accent his point.

At the lakeshore the Utes halted. A short exchange resulted in two of the warriors forcing Winona, Evelyn, and Lou to sit down. Winona couldn't take her eyes off her mate. In his condition it wouldn't take much to smother the weak spark of life that remained.

To Winona's utter horror, the Utes must have had the same thought. For the next moment, without any forewarning, the tall Ute and one other carried Nate into the lake and lowered him into the cold water.

They were drowning him!

Touch the Clouds's superb physique had always served him well. As the huge boulder obliterated half the sky, he slapped his legs against the sorrel and raced forward. At the same time, he bellowed to Drags the Rope and the others. The narrow defile pealed to rumbling thunder caused by the boulder bouncing off the wall. Frantic shouts and panicked whinnies added to the din.

A shadow enveloped Touch the Clouds and his warhorse. Doom was upon them. He expected to be crushed to a pulp, and he tensed for the imminent impact. Drags the Rope called out to him, but the yell was eclipsed by a tremendous, nigh-deafening crash. The walls shook and the ground quaked, and a billowing, roiling cloud rose to fill the gap with choking dust.

Touch the Clouds didn't rein up until he reached the next bend. He turned to look back, but he could barely see his hand at arm's length, so thick was the dust cloud. Out of it a silhouette took substance.

Drags the Rope reined up, coughing and sputtering. His hair, his face, his clothes were caked with dust.

"You made it safely too!" Touch the Clouds's relief was boundless. To lose his best friend would sadden him beyond measure, a sorrow he would endure for the rest of his life.

"The boulder landed right behind me," Drags the Rope said between coughs. "I heard a scream."

"We must check on the others." Touch the Clouds tried to dismount, but there wasn't enough room. He could barely squeeze a leg between the rock wall and his sorrel. "We need to find a place where we can climb down," he said, and goaded his horse around the bend. As luck would have it, the defile widened slightly, enough to permit them to dismount. On foot, the two of them hastened back.

The cloud still hung in the air, thick with fine particles. Touch the Clouds covered his mouth with one hand and cautiously advanced. He couldn't see the rim, couldn't see the walls close beside him. His right foot bumped a fist-size fragment of rock, the first of many. Carefully stepping over them, he groped for the boulder.

The tip of his left foot struck an object that felt different from the debris, something soft and yielding. Crouching, Touch the Clouds ran his hand over it and was appalled to discover it was the head of a horse twisted at an unnatural angle. His questing fingers roved along the animal's blood-drenched neck, which was nearly as flat as a leaf, and made contact with the boulder.

Touch the Clouds bowed his head in sorrow. The rest of

the horse, and whoever had been riding it, were underneath.

Drags the Rope edged next to him. "This must be Shoulder Blade. He was next behind me."

The deformed warrior had been another close friend. Swallowing hard, Touch the Clouds raised his head to shout, but someone on the other side of the boulder beat him to it.

"Touch the Clouds! Drags the Rope! Can you hear me? This is Six Feathers!"

"We are alive and unhurt!" Touch the Clouds responded. "But we cannot say the same of Shoulder Blade!"

"We know! He and Buffalo Hump were crushed. Buffalo Hump's legs are sticking out on this side! They just stopped twitching!"

"Everyone else is all right? No other horses were hurt?"

"Not a scratch. But we cannot go on. We must back our horses out and find a way around."

"No!" Touch the Clouds straightened. "Get out quickly in case more boulders fall, and wait for us." He would not risk losing more warriors. And he could not stop thinking about the shadow that flitted around the rim moments before the boulder came tumbling down.

"We will do as you say," Six Feathers answered.

"Hurry!" Touch the Clouds heeded his own advice. Spinning, he grabbed Drags the Rope by the elbow and hustled toward the bend. The rim was still obscured by the cloud, but it wouldn't be for long.

"Do you hear that?" Drags the Rope suddenly asked.

From above drifted a grating noise, as of stone scraping on stone. "Run!" Touch the Clouds urged, and did so, just as another rumbling roar reverberated in the defile. Another boulder was falling! Or, more accurately, had been pushed! Touch the Clouds looked up, but he couldn't tell whether it was behind them, in front of them, or directly above them. He ran faster. The bend couldn't be far, and once they were around it they would be safe.

The rumbling swelled until it was like the rumbling a great herd of buffalo made when they stampeded. At its crescendo came an earth-shaking crash louder than the first. The earth under Touch the Clouds's moccasins buckled and he was pitched onto his stomach. A gust of wind fanned the back of his neck, and then the ravine grew as dark as twilight. A second, denser cloud of dust had been added to the first.

Touch the Clouds began to rise. Inadvertently, he inhaled, and promptly regretted it. It felt as if he had sucked a handful of sand into his mouth. Dust layered his tongue, his throat. An irresistible impulse to gag doubled him over. He coughed uncontrollably. Thrusting a hand over his mouth, he breathed shallow to avoid a repeat of his mistake. Gradually, he recovered enough to stand and go on.

Only now it was dark as pitch. Touch The Clouds blinked to clear his eyes of stinging particles, but it didn't help. Holding his right arm across his forehead to shield them, he called out, "Drags the Rope?" From close ahead came a muffled response. He advanced by sliding each foot a knife's length at a time. "Where are you?"

"Here."

Touch the Clouds bent and groped with both hands. Fingers clutched his. Squatting, he ran his left hand along his friend's arm. "Are you hurt?"

"I tripped and struck my head on the wall. I feel weak. And dizzy."

"Do not move." Touch the Clouds slid his hand up across Drags the Rope's cheek, forehead, and hair. There was a damp spot, but the flow of blood appeared to have stopped. "We must get you out." Touch the Clouds couldn't tell more until they were in sunlight. "Lean on me. We will walk sideways, and I will bear your weight."

Drags the Rope groaned as he was assisted to his feet. "The boulder almost crushed us like the other did Shoulder Blade."

Cold fury bubbled in Touch the Clouds at the thought of

how close they had come to a grisly end. Holding his free arm in front of him, he steered them around the bend to where they had left the horses. Both animals were gone.

Drags the Rope was slumped against him. "They were scared and ran off," he commented. "Let us hope they do not run all the way back to our village."

"No more talking until we are out," Touch the Clouds whispered. It had occurred to him that whoever was rolling boulders down on them might hear them and try again. As cautiously as if they were treading barefoot on shards of broken glass, they went on. The dust cloud slowly thinned and breathing became easier. Once past another bend, the ravine widened considerably. Visibility improved. Touch the Clouds scanned the high ramparts, but no more shadows appeared.

Soon the ravine ended. An arrow's flight away were their horses. Touch the Clouds sat his friend on a small boulder and examined the wound. There was a gash as long as his thumb and half as wide above one ear. "You will mend and be your old self," he predicted.

"Already I feel much better," Drags the Rope said. "We can look for the Crow camp whenever you want."

"Rest awhile. I have something else to do first." Touch the Clouds brought their horses over, mounted the sorrel, and rode to a bare slope that brought him to the top of the ravine. As he climbed he notched an arrow to his bow. He hoped those responsible were still there. But he should have known better.

Dozens of footprints marked the spot. A pair of long poles, used to lever the boulders, had been left behind.

Touch the Clouds swung down. The tracks were moccasin prints. Since no two tribes fashioned their footwear exactly alike, a competent tracker could always tell them apart.

"Crows," Touch the Clouds said, and his giant body shook with rage.

It was time to go to war.

Chapter Ten

Winona King had felt fear before, but never fear like this. Never fear so potent it paralyzed her limbs and her vocal cords. Never fear so chilling her heart was a solid block of ice. The Utes were drowning the man she loved! Sadistically, callously, submerging him under the cold mountain water! She saw his legs go under, his hips and his chest. She saw his chin disappear. His mouth. His nose. And a terrible, fierce bloodlust seized her. Before she knew what she was doing, Winona had heaved to her feet.

The Ute with the lance bleated in surprise and turned to stop her, but Winona refused to be deterred. Lowering her head, she butted into him like a bighorn sheep into a cougar. He doubled over and tottered, and several more strides brought her to the water's edge.

The fourth Ute rushed up and snatched at her shoulder. Whirling, Winona kicked him where it would hurt a man

135

the most. His features flushed crimson and he, too, stumbled aside.

Growling like an animal gone berserk, Winona waded into the water. With her hands bound she was hampered in what she could do, but she had to do *something*. She would use her head, her shoulders, her teeth, her legs. She would save her husband no matter what.

The tall Ute let go of Nate and moved to intercept her. He had left his war club on shore but still had a bone-handled knife in a sheath on his right hip. Surprisingly, he made no attempt to draw it, but extended his arms and signed, "Stop!"

Winona was too incensed to heed. Lowering her head, she tried to butt him as she had the warrior with the lance. She couldn't move as fast in the water, though, and the tall Ute sidestepped and seized her around the waist, stopping her dead.

"Let go of me!" Winona fumed in Shoshone. She kicked at his shins and knees, but the water rendered her efforts impotent.

The tall Ute held on tighter. He spoke softly, soothingly, as if seeking to calm her, but Winona refused to be calmed. She thrashed and bucked and kicked until fatigue left her spent and limp. Only then did the tall Ute let go and stand back. "Stay calm," he signed.

Winona would do no such thing. Girding herself, she prepared to renew her assault.

The tall Ute's fingers rippled in more sign. While the symbols most tribes used were relatively few in number, no more than several hundred all told, a skilled sign talker, by combining the symbols in all manner of ways, was able to get across any meaning he or she desired. The tall Ute was quite skilled, and his statements translated into, "You are wrong to attack us, Wife-of-Grizzly-Killer. We do not mean you or your family harm."

"You speak with two tongues!" Winona snapped in Shoshone.

"I can tell you do not believe me," the tall Ute signed. "But my words are true. We tied you and the girls to keep you from being hurt. I knew you would object to my plan to help your husband."

Winona glanced past him. The other Ute had one arm under Nate's head and was holding it above water so Nate could breathe.

"I am Neota. If you promise to control yourself, I will cut you free," the tall Ute signed. "Nod if you agree."

Confused, uncertain, Winona fought down her desire to throw herself at him and nodded. He drew his knife, stepped around behind her, and sliced the strip with a single practiced stroke. For a moment the tip of his blade was close to her back, and she could not keep from flinching.

Neota replaced his blade. "Remember your promise." He waded to Nate and placed his right palm on Nate's chest, above the heart. Then he signed, "Grizzly Killer is as strong as a bull buffalo. Once the fever leaves him he will recover quickly."

"I thought you intended to drown him," Winona signed.

Smiling, Neota responded, "My grandfather was attacked by a grizzly when I was seven winters old. His wounds became infected and he had a fever as bad as your husband's. Nothing my mother or my grandmother did helped, so they went to a healer, who told them to dip my grandfather in the lake near our village five times a day, which they did. By the afternoon of the second day his fever broke, and from that day on he grew strong."

Winona looked down at her own legs, which were growing chill. *The lake! Why hadn't she thought of it?* Submersion for brief periods would help lower Nate's temperature and *keep* it low.

"There is a risk," Neota continued. "Sometimes the fever leaves but the person becomes sick and must stay in bed for many sleeps. The secret to prevent that is to give them a lot of hot tea as soon as the fever is gone."

"All you wanted to do was help?" Winona marveled.

"My people and your husband smoked the pipe of peace, and my people do not break their word. For as long as the sun endures we will not lift a finger against him, or against his family."

"Why did you not tell me this sooner?"

"You did not give me the chance," Neota answered. "And you would not have believed me if I had." He nodded at Nate. "It was wiser to *show* you. Now you may cut your daughter and the white girl loose. Have them bring blankets and heat tea. We never know when the fever will break, and we must be ready."

Winona clasped his hand, then signed, "You have earned a friend for life. If I, or my family, can ever be of help to you or your family, we will drop whatever we are doing and come to your aid."

"Your promise means more to me than you can know at this moment." Warmth radiated from the Ute's kindly eyes. "I have heard it said the wife of Grizzly Killer is a worthy mate for one so famous and feared. From this day on, when he is mentioned, I will tell all those I know it is true."

Evelyn and Louisa were fidgeting as if ants were in their clothes, eager to be free. The Ute with the lance lent Winona his knife so she could oblige them. "You saw what Neota signed," she said in English. "Blue Flower, put water on to boil. Lou, bring as many blankets as you can carry. I will stay with Nate."

"Will do, Ma," Evelyn said.

"Blankets aren't all I'll bring," Louisa stated. "Maybe you trust these gents, but your own son taught me to never trust anyone except Shoshones."

Daughter and daughter-in-law bolted up the path to do her bidding, and Winona, reversing her grip on the knife, returned it to the lender.

The youngest of the four, he couldn't be more than eighteen, if that. As he accepted his weapon, he motioned at Evelyn's and Louisa's rapidly retreating figures. "How many winters has your daughter seen?" he signed.

"Twelve, almost thirteen," Winona absently answered. "Why do you ask?"

"She has a fighting heart. She will be a good wife to the warrior who takes her into his lodge."

Winona bunched her fists in indignation. How dare he talk about her daughter like that! It would be quite a few winters yet before Blue Flower was old enough to wed. Winona was on the verge of giving him a piece of her mind when it occurred to her that Shoshone girls often wed at sixteen, some even younger. Her daughter was closer to marrying age than she liked to admit.

"I am Niwot. Remember me. I will come back in three winters and ask her if she would like to be my woman."

It was all Winona could do not to slug him for his arrogance. Motherly love struggled with uncomfortable reality. Both were forgotten when Nate groaned. Whirling, she waded out. "I would be happy to help hold him," she signed to Neota, who politely stepped aside so she could step in close.

"We cannot keep him in this cold water much longer," the Ute signed. "We must take him out and warm him so his blood keeps flowing. Then we will bring him back in and do it all over again."

Winona prayed the idea worked. The arrival of the Utes was an answer to her spirit's innermost plea. Sliding her left hand under her man's shoulder, she gently touched his cheek. "Live, my husband," she pleaded. *"Live."*

Drags the Rope was on his horse, waiting, when Touch the Clouds returned from the top of the ravine. "What did you find?"

Touch the Clouds told him.

"So they were Crows, after all? I had begun to suspect otherwise."

Touch the Clouds had established that three Crows were involved, and that after rolling the boulders off the rim, they had scaled a slope to the south too steep and treacherous for the sorrel to negotiate.

Drags the Rope scanned the broad canyon before them. "The Crow camp must be close by, as the trader claimed." He slid an arrow from his quiver and nocked it to his bow. "Perhaps they are watching us as we speak."

Touch the Clouds kneed his sorrel, taking the lead. Cottonwoods lined a tiny creek on the right. On the left was open ground dotted by random patches of brush. He saw sparrows and a raven and a rattlesnake sunning itself. He saw the tracks of deer, the tracks of a bobcat, and the tracks of a bear. The one thing he did not see were human tracks, nor any evidence anyone had been there before them.

"Most perplexing," Drags the Rope remarked. "Where can the Crows be?"

A thorough search confirmed the canyon was empty save for wildlife. Touch the Clouds drew rein at the far end and rubbed his chin. Something was wrong, very wrong. According to Borke, the Crow camp should be there. And he had seen Crow tracks atop the ravine with his own eyes. Where, then, were they?

Drags the Rope was having similar doubts. "No Crow would camp here. There is not enough grass for grazing."

"And only the one way in and out," Touch the Clouds observed. In their circuit of the canyon he had not seen another.

"Are you saying we are trapped in here?" Drags the Rope said in alarm.

"Let us find out."

They scoured the base of the encircling canyon walls on the south side. Nowhere was there a break. Nowhere a means to the top. They crossed the creek and found themselves back at the mouth of the defile that had brought them there. Touch the Clouds almost stopped. He thought he heard faint, distant shouts, but when he listened closely, all he heard was the sigh of the wind.

To the north was more of the same—an unbroken sheet of rock carved ages ago by a mighty upheaval. Lofty crags too sheer to climb posed an insurmountable barrier to the outside world.

"Eventually we will starve," Drags the Rope said. "There is not enough game to last us forever."

The comment gave Touch the Clouds food for thought. He had seen a lot of deer tracks, more than there should be in so isolated a spot. The only way to account for it was if there was another way in and out, a way deer would be more prone to use than the narrow gap through the rock ramparts. "Do not give up hope. We will keep looking."

Cracks laced the canyon walls. Some were hairline thin, some a lot wider. None penetrated very deep into the cliff face. So when Touch the Clouds came abreast of one mired in shadow and felt a puff of air on his cheek, his curiosity was piqued. Nudging the sorrel nearer, he peered in. The opening was wide enough to admit a horse. Just beyond it widened even more, enough to accommodate several buffalo walking abreast. "Coming?" he asked, and kneed the sorrel in.

"Will it lead us out?"

"If it does not, we will be no worse off than we are now."

Touch the Clouds was encouraged by the fact that the dirt was pockmarked by tracks, mainly those of deer but also others. They came to a bend, and beyond it the cleft became twice as wide, wide enough for their entire war party to ride through shoulder-to-shoulder. In short order Touch the Clouds emerged into the bright glare of the midday sun. By his reckoning they weren't all that far from the defile in which they had nearly been killed.

Drags the Rope was also scanning the ground. "All these

David Thompson

tracks, but not one made by a horse. The Crows were never in that canyon."

"Yet I saw Crow footprints," Touch the Clouds reminded him. "They must be somewhere close by."

"Perhaps it was an honest mistake," Drags the Rope ventured. "Most whites are like infants in the wild. They do not know where they have been after they have been there."

How true that was. Touch the Clouds remembered a young trapper he met at the King lodge, a youth who couldn't tell east from west or north from south. Shoshones learned to tell direction when they were small children; they had to in order to survive. But not whites. Incredibly, they could go their whole lives long in complete ignorance.

Nate told the young man the mountains were no place for him, that he should go back across the prairie to his home. But the young trapper refused. Not long after, he joined a trapping brigade, and while out laying traps, he became lost, strayed into Blackfoot territory, and was brutally slain.

At a trot, Touch the Clouds and Drags the Rope went to find their companions. Touch the Clouds expected them to be at the mouth of the defile, and they didn't disappoint him. Four warriors were guarding the horses, and they came running excitedly.

"You are alive!" exclaimed Runs Behind. "We had given you up for dead!"

"Where are the rest?" Touch the Clouds slid down.

Runs Behind nodded toward the opening. "Six Feathers said we could not return to our village without knowing for certain. They went back in to try and find you."

Touch the Clouds handed his reins to Drags the Rope. "I will go in alone." His friend claimed to be all right, but Touch the Clouds had seen him grimace a few times on the way there. The gash had to be bothering him more than Drags the Rope admitted.

Ten steps in, Touch the Clouds abruptly stopped. A feel-

142

ing of being closed in came over him, of being smothered. He experienced a blind spike of panic that the walls were about to come crashing down on top of him. Involuntarily, he glanced up. His pulse quickened, his throat constricted.

Gradually the panic faded and Touch the Clouds went on. He was mad at himself for his lapse. It was unbefitting a warrior. From up ahead rose voices, and around the next turn he saw Six Feathers and the rest, packed close to the first giant boulder. Several warriors were boosting Six Feathers, but he couldn't quite grip the top. The surface was too smooth.

No one noticed Touch the Clouds. Grinning, he folded his huge arms and quipped, "If this is your idea of a rescue, I would be long dead before you reached me."

Peals of happiness and laughter greeted the discovery that he was alive. They rushed to him, and those nearest clapped him on the chest and congratulated him on his narrow escape. Six Feathers squeezed through to place a hand on his shoulder. "My heart sings, giant one. I was afraid I must bear the terrible news to your family."

"It was not my day to die." Touch the Clouds gazed at the upturned faces, all burnished the color of copper, and realized three members of their party were missing. "Where are the whites?"

"They rode off before the dust settled," Six Feathers said. "I guess they thought you had been slain. I tried to persuade them to help, but they could not understand me and I could not understand them."

Touch the Clouds was in a somber mood as he led the war party south. Artemis Borke had been much too quick to dismiss him as dead. A pattern was becoming clear, a pattern of deliberate deception, and worse. He tried assuring himself he must be wrong. He had to be misreading the signs. Yet the inconsistencies nagged at him like a shrewish wife. Was it coincidence that the two Crows who attacked the village happened to slay Hungry Wolf, the most vocal critic of the trading post? Was it coincidence that Borke showed up so soon after and claimed that the new Hawkens used by the Crows had been stolen? Was it a coincidence that Borke then lured them into a trap where Crows were waiting to roll boulders down on their heads?

So many questions, and Touch the Clouds was determined to find the answers. If his growing suspicions were borne out, the long-standing Shoshone taboo against shedding white blood would soon be broken.

And if war with the whites resulted, so be it.

Zachary King had learned to go long spells without sleep, but he had been in the saddle for over thirty-six hours and his eyelids were as heavy as his cabin. Repeatedly, he gave himself a vigorous shake to keep from drifting off. They had covered a lot of ground, much more than he thought they would in that amount of time despite the delay caused by the grizzly, and now they were only four or five hours from the Green River.

So close, yet so far. Zach longed to push on through, but the smart thing to do was rest a spell. The dun was flecked with sweat and breathing much too heavily. For its sake, as much as his own, Zach looked for a likely spot and found it in the shade of a towering oak beside a small spring.

Zach was thirsty enough to gulp a gallon, but he was savvy enough to limit himself to a few handfuls. He had to watch the dun, though. Left on its own, it would drink so much it would flounder. So after it drank what he deemed was enough, he led it to the far side of the oak and picketed it with a makeshift stake he fashioned from a broken piece of tree limb. Satisfied it wasn't going anywhere, Zach sat with his back to the tree trunk.

The terrain ahead wasn't as rugged. Once he was across the next ridge, he would be within sight of the emerald hills bordering the Green River valley, a verdant paradise for man and beast. In olden days it had been the site of most of the annual rendezvous.

Zach always liked attending the rendezvous, where traders from St. Louis and elsewhere displayed marvelous items for sale or barter. It had been a wonderland of sights, scents, and sounds to a small boy his age. Not until he was in his teens had he learned that the traders invariably charged five to ten times what the items were worth. The traders claimed that they needed to charge so high to cover their expenses. More cynical sorts claimed it was done to fleece the hard-working trappers out of their hard-earned money.

Another aspect to the rendezvous that Zach always enjoyed was visiting the encampments of the peaceful tribes who attended. The Shoshones, the Flatheads, the Nez Percé, and others made it a point to show up for the same reason the trappers did—the trade goods.

And for the socializing. The trappers spent their days wrestling, wagering on horse races, conducting footraces, and holding shooting matches. Nights were for card-playing, dice-playing, womanizing, and drinking. Especially drinking. Mountaineers prided themselves on their capacity for alcohol; drinking challengers under the table was a common sport.

The years flew by, and the fur trade withered. Easterners had taken a fancy to silk and beaver was no longer in feverish demand. Hundreds of trappers were left jobless. Some, like Zach's pa, married Indian women and stayed on, living much like the Indians did. Others drifted to California or the Oregon Country. A few returned to the mundane lives they were stuck in before answering the call of the wild, but not many. After tasting true freedom, after sampling adventure and excitement, city life was much too tame. Men who had scaled mile-high peaks and ridden like the wind from scalp-hungry hostiles couldn't abide the notion of spending the rest of their years chained to a desk or held prisoner behind a store counter.

David Thompson

Zach understood why. He could no more give up the life he lived than he could give up life itself. His pa once told him people were molded by the world around them until they became part of that world. If that was true, it explained his love for the mountains and prairies. The wilderness was in his blood. Civilized life held no appeal whatsoever. Zach could never understand men willing to exist in daily drudgery. They traded their freedom for security. Adventure for boredom. They became, in effect, slaves to their own timidity.

Maybe, in a way, that was just as well for their welfare. The wilderness wasn't for the faint of heart. Living in the mountains was a never-ending struggle for survival, for food to put on the table, for the clothes on one's back, for all the little things those who lived in the false world of cities and towns took for granted.

The real world, Nature's world, the world of fang and claw, didn't pamper. The real world didn't coddle. The real world was a fiery forge in which human steel was tempered to razor sharpness. Those who couldn't stand the heat were better off going back to the false world of civilization. It cushioned them from reality. It blunted those who lived its lie, turning men into timid, overfed sheep.

Closing his eyes, Zach felt the tension drain from him like water down a sieve. It was nice to relax for a while, nice to catch his breath before the next stage of his journey. The last stage, barring a mishap. He should reach Touch the Clouds's village by sunset. A quick meal, a short rest, and he would be on his way back to his father's cabin, either with the healer, Raven's Wing, or whatever medicine she whipped up to help him.

Zach King dozed. To a casual observer he might appear defenseless and easy to pick off. But years of peril-filled scrapes had conditioned him to awaken at the slightest foreign sound. When a soft *crunch*, barely audible, fluttered on the breeze, Zach snapped instantly awake. His instinctive response was to lift his head and look around, but he refrained. Instead, cracking his eyelids, he peered toward a stand of saplings and brush thirty yards away.

Zach didn't want whoever or whatever it was to realize he was onto them. Movement registered. Something was in there, all right, something bigger than a bobcat but smaller than a buffalo.

Weeds framed a painted face. It was there, and it was gone, but the brief glimpse was enough to reveal that Zach was being stalked by a Crow war party. *Crows, in Shoshone country!*

Zach held his mother's people in high esteem, much more so than the esteem he bestowed on whites. The Shoshones were more accepting of him, more tolerant, although there were those who treated him with contempt for the same reason most whites did—the fact that he was of mixed blood. But that didn't matter at the moment. As an adopted Shoshone, he had a responsibility to them to slay or drive off their enemies.

Another Crow's image sprouted out of the greenery, then yet another, and another, until they were nine in number. They were slowly working closer so they could jump him, spreading out as they came.

Zach's Hawken was across his thighs, his right thumb on the hammer. He had an urge to shoot, but if he did the Crows would cut him down before he could reach the dun. Cleverness was called for. Slowly sitting up, he made a show of yawning. The Crows all went to ground. They wouldn't pincushion him with arrows so long as they felt they had a chance to take him alive. He made it a point not to look in their direction. Not directly, anyhow, but he did watch them out of the corner of his eye as he walked around the tree and over toward his horse. He patted its neck, then turned away as he had no intention of leaving just yet.

Untying the stake would take too long and alert the Crow to his true intent. Their dark eyes aglitter with sadistic delight, they were waiting for him to stray to the spring so they could pounce. They had him, or believed they did.

Hiking his arms as if he were about to stretch, Zach suddenly bent and yanked on the top of the stake. It wasn't embedded that deep and popped right out. A lithe bound carried him to the dun, and he was on it and galloping off before the Crows recovered their collective wits.

Howls of frustration greeted the ploy. The Crows bounded in pursuit but soon realized it was pointless. Several arrows were loosed, but they missed. One Crow hurled a lance that fell well short. At a shout from a stocky warrior, they wheeled and sped back into the trees after their own mounts.

Zach veered toward a tree-cloaked hill. They outnumbered him, but he had an advantage in another, more important, regard. He had been through this area many times. He knew the lay of the land better than they. And just as a wily fox put the terrain to best use when chased by hounds, so would he use the terrain to outwit the Crows.

The hill was a ways off when the war party broke from cover, hot after his hide. Zach looked back and grinned in defiance, eliciting a new round of howls and whoops. He had a good lead, but not enough to guarantee success. To increase his odds, he whipped his Hawken to his shoulder, steadied the barrel as best he could, curled back the hammer, and fired.

A Crow at the front of the pack was caught high in the shoulder and flung into the grass. He rolled a dozen feet before he came to a stop. Pushing onto his knees, he placed a hand over the bleeding bullet hole and swayed.

The other Crows did exactly as Zach had hoped. They drew rein and wheeled to go to their brother's aid.

His grin widening, Zach raced around the pine-covered hill to give the impression that he was hell-bent on fleeing. But the moment he was out of sight, he reined into the trees.

Into the deepest shadow he could find. Swiftly reloading, he bent low over the dun.

It took the Crows close to fifteen minutes to dig the slug out of their wounded companion and apply a strip of buckskin as a bandage. In a close knot they trotted into view, traveling to the northwest. They wrongly assumed that Zach was too far ahead for them to catch, and they were now on their way to wherever they had been heading when he stumbled onto them.

To the northwest lay the Green River region—and Touch the Clouds's village.

"Just as I reckoned," Zach growled. He waited until they were out of sight, then followed. Unless he missed his guess, they were bent on lifting Shoshone scalps. But he would be damned if he let them hurt his kin. The hunters had just become the hunted.

Chapter Eleven

Touch the Clouds and the Shoshone war party paralleled the fresh tracks left by Artemis Borke and his two friends on their way to the trading post. Touch the Clouds assumed that the whites would ride straight through, so he was more than a little puzzled and curious when the three men halted in a small clearing a third of the distance there.

The reason became evident when more tracks were discovered. Three riders on unshod horses had trotted down off a nearby mountain to the same clearing. Then all seven had gone on together at a leisurely gait.

Touch the Clouds found it extremely interesting that the mountain happened to flank the defile where Shoulder Blade and Buffalo Hump lost their lives. His suspicions, and his anger, climbed. Whites rarely rode unshod animals. Which meant the three newcomers were Indians, and must be the Crows who had pushed the boulders down onto his friends. It was apparent the Crows and the whites were working together.

But why? Touch the Clouds reflected. What did the whites hope to gain? Why go to so much trouble to establish a trading post in Shoshone territory and then ally themselves with Shoshone enemies? What could Borke gain by an alliance with the Crows that he couldn't through an alliance with the Shoshones? It made no sense. But then, much of what white men did defied understanding. They were a wild, reckless, mystifying people, tireless in their quest to line their pockets, as Nate King once described it. It was money that brought them flocking to the mountains in search of beaver. It had to be money that brought these traders now. To whites, becoming rich was the dream of dreams.

It followed, then, that there must be a secret motive behind Borke's dealings with the Crows. A motive that involved making money. But in their greed the whites had committed a grievous mistake. Touch the Clouds's people wouldn't stand for having a trading post in their territory that did business with tribes out for their blood.

As usual, Drags the Rope was thinking in a similar vein. "What will we do when we reach the post? Wipe the whites out?"

The question was a weighty one. Touch the Clouds's decision could impact the Shoshones for generations to come. For the Shoshones to take a white life, even if provoked, might invite violent reprisals. "We will demand an explanation from Artemis Borke," he replied.

"Is that enough? When we both know Borke speaks with two tongues? He has misled us from the beginning."

"What would you recommend?"

"Escort the whites from our land. Order them never to return. Then send word to Grizzly Killer. Invite him to sit at council with our elders. He is uniquely fitted to help us preserve peace with his kind, and his advice will be invaluable."

As always, Drags the Rope was to be commended for his wisdom, and Touch the Clouds did so. He wished Grizzly Killer were with them at that moment. Who better to see into the heart of a white man than another white man? Nate would have seen through Borke from the beginning and spared the Shoshone people profound misery.

The sun was well on its westward arc when a broad green belt of lush vegetation betokened their arrival at the Green River valley. Soon they would reach Dead Elk Creek. From the tracks, Touch the Clouds could tell Borke's group wasn't far ahead. Signaling for the other warriors to halt, he told Six Feathers to hold them there while he went on ahead with Drags the Rope.

Touch the Clouds wanted to see for himself. He had to witness the whites and the Crows together so there would be no doubt whatsoever. Accordingly, he raced on at a gallop until he came to a wooded slope. He could hear his quarry below, winding lower. They would come out near the rear of the trading post.

Slanting to the left, Touch the Clouds sped along a rise to a vantage point that gave him an unobstructed view of the valley floor. Soon a column of horsemen filed from the trees. Six in all, with Artemis Borke at their head.

"Do you see what I see?" Drags the Rope whispered.

All six were white men. Men Touch the Clouds had seen before. Men from the trading post. Three wore moccasins, not their customary boots, and were riding bareback. Riding Indian horses, animals the whites had acquired in trade.

"Somehow Borke obtained Crow moccasins and had his men wear them to put the blame on the Crows," Drags the Rope summed up the wily trader's plot.

Touch the Clouds grunted his agreement. That much was obvious. But the crucial question still remained: *Why?* Why had Borke gone to such extraordinary lengths to try and slay him? Was it his stand on the sale of firewater? Was Borke that greedy? That petty?

A hail rose from the tower. The sentry grinned and waved, and Artemis Borke responded in kind. Quickly climbing down a ladder, the sentry opened the gate. Amid lusty shouts, Borke and the others drew rein in front of the corral and swung down. The men wearing moccasins tramped into their living quarters and reemerged after a bit wearing boots, at which point everyone except the sentry flocked into the post. Soon rowdy laughter and gruff singing filled the compound.

Drags the Rope's jaw was sculpted from quartz. "I do not know why they turned on us, and I do not care. We cannot let this stand. If we do, word will spread and whites everywhere will think we are weak."

The comment ignited Touch the Clouds's memory. Of a time at a rendezvous when a whiskey-soaked trapper had bumped into him. The man had bristled like a porcupine, grabbed him by the front of the shirt, and spewed oaths as foreign to Touch the Clouds as the language of the Comanches or Apaches. He had been more amused than anything else. The trapper, a feisty badger of a man notorious for his temper, was barely as tall as his chest. Touch the Clouds could have swatted him like a fly. But in keeping with the Shoshone practice of always treating whites decently, he had refrained.

Emboldened, the trapper had drawn back a hand to slap him. But the blow never landed. Nate King saw to that. He dashed out of nowhere and slugged the trapper on the jaw. They left the man lying in the dirt.

"Don't ever let no-accounts like that walk over you," Nate had said. "Never show weakness, or they'll pick on you every chance they get. The only thing they respect is strength. Be strong when you need to be, whether they're white or not."

Whether they're white or not. Touch the Clouds shifted

toward Drags the Rope. "Bring Six Feathers and the others. We will—" He stopped, for more riders were approaching from across Dead Elk Creek. And this time there could be no doubt. They were definitely Crows. Nine in number, and one appeared to be wounded.

"Those dogs dare to invade our land!" Drags the Rope exclaimed.

As boldly as could be, the Crows rode straight to the palisade. The sentry didn't act the least bit surprised. When he hollered, out of the main building rushed Artemis Borke and a majority of the other whites. The gate was pulled wide to admit their visitors. Stepping forward, Borke greeted the Crows warmly—in sign language.

"I was not aware he knew sign."

Nor was Touch the Clouds. It was yet another of the many secrets the trader had kept from them.

Borke invited the Crows into the main buildings. All but one accepted. The last warrior stayed with the horses, proof the Crows didn't trust the whites completely. How ironic, Touch the Clouds thought, that his enemies displayed more intelligence than he had. "Ride and bring the rest. We are going to show Borke and these Crows that they have made the worst mistake of their lives."

Sliding off his sorrel, Touch the Clouds wrapped the reins around a low tree limb and moved to a nearby log to sit. He couldn't get over how gullible he had been. How foolhardy. He thought having a trading post would benefit his people. Instead, its presence had brought nothing but heartache and trouble.

Touch the Clouds had learned an important lesson. Never again would he take white men at their word. They must prove they were worthy of his trust.

The sentry was making a circuit of the tower. Another couple of steps and he faced toward the rise.

Touch the Clouds wasn't worried about being spotted. At that distance his buckskins blended perfectly into the underbrush. No one could spot him. Or so he imagined.

It made his shock doubly great when the cool metal of a gun muzzle was pressed against the back of his neck.

Zach King had been following the Crows for over half an hour when he stealthily began to narrow the distance. He planned to pick them off one by one until every last invader was dead or had fled for home. They were moving at a trot, the wounded man gamely holding his own. Few ever glanced back; their attention was on the land ahead.

Zach drew within rifle range and brought the dun to a stop. Tucking his Hawken to his shoulder, he took deliberate aim. Some people had compunctions about shooting another person in the back. Not him. Killing was killing. The Crows wouldn't hesitate to turn him into maggot bait any way they could. Why should he be any different?

At the very instant Zach's finger curled around the trigger, the Crows abruptly slanted to the northwest. If they held to that course they would give Touch the Clouds's village a wide berth.

Zach slowly lowered his rifle. Maybe the Crows were leaving Shoshone territory, in which case it would be pointless to tangle with them. To be safe, he elected to follow a while yet. The decision, though, ate at him like a wolverine chewing on his innards. It would delay him in reaching the healer, delay him in returning to his parents' cabin with the medicine. But it also might save untold lives if the Crows were working their way around to come at Touch the Clouds's village from a different direction. He would give them another hour. By then it should be apparent what they were up to.

Only half that amount had gone by when the Crows descended toward a tributary of the Green.

Zach slowly approached the crest of a ridge to avoid silhouetting himself against the ridgeline. One peek satisfied him that the Crows were well below him. He was about to slip over the rim when he saw where they were bound. Bewilderment froze him with the reins half raised.

On the other side of Dead Elk Creek stood a structure that had not been there six months before. It was a post of some kind, complete with palisades and a guard tower.

Keeping the ridge between him and the lookout, Zach circled for a closer inspection. The Shoshones would want to hear about this. And his father, too, once his pa was on the mend. The thought speared him with remorse. He had squandered too much time already. The Shoshones were safe enough for the time being, so inspecting the fort could wait. He would continue on to the Green and find Raven's Wing.

A hint of movement gave Zach pause. A hundred yards away a rider was hurrying to the north. Much closer than that a lone figure in buckskins crept through the vegetation, his gaze cemented on the guard tower.

Bringing the dun to a stop, Zach left it there and cat-footed to a spot above and behind the crouching warrior. A tingle ran through him. A surge of excitement at the prospect of doing something he had never done before. As silently as a ghost, he stalked forward, expecting at any second for the figure in buckskins to hear or sense him, and turn.

Zach almost laughed aloud as he touched the end of the Hawken's barrel to the warrior's neck and joked in his mother's tongue, "Does the mightiest Shoshone who ever lived have plugs of wax in his ears?"

Touch the Clouds rose and spun. Smiling warmly, he clapped a hand the size of a ham on Zach's shoulder. "Stalking Coyote! I cannot describe how happy I am to see you again. You could not have come at a better time."

"I followed the Crows," Zach related, with a nod at the fort. "What are you doing here? What has been going on?"

"Where do I begin?"

The giant warrior's account kindled anger that gradually

156

flared to red-hot fury. Zach had known Hungry Wolf, Wallowing Bull, and Buffalo Hump extremely well. They were childhood friends, and he had spent many an hour hunting and cavorting in their company. He had also shared meals with Shoulder Blade, one of the kindest warriors he ever met.

"Soon Drags the Rope and the others will join us and we must decide on a course of action," Touch the Clouds concluded. "We cannot let this go on."

"I agree," Zach said. "But there's nothing to decide. Let me deal with them."

Touch the Clouds's eyes narrowed. "I have known you since the morning you were born, Stalking Coyote. I know how much you like to count coup. So I must caution you. We want to punish these whites, but we do not want a war."

"Oh, we'll punish them, sure enough," Zach said in English. In Shoshone he responded, "Do not fear."

Zach refrained from mentioning that in his opinion the Shoshones had brought the bloodshed down on their own heads. They were always so willing to bend over backward for whites. They had to learn to take a stand and not let themselves be pushed around.

"It is unfortunate your father is not here," Touch the Clouds commented. "We could use his advice."

"I can handle this as well as Pa," Zach said a tad defensively. Always being compared to his pa used to rankle him until he realized the comparisons were compliments. "We will wait until dark and then pay Mr. Artemis Borke and his friends a visit. I will tend to the whites. You and your warriors can deal with the Crows."

"I can trust you, Stalking Coyote?"

"The Shoshones are my people too. The last thing I want is to bring trouble down on their heads."

"For all our sakes, I hope so."

*   *   *

David Thompson

A gray fog blanketed him. Everywhere he looked it was the same. He took a stumbling step, his legs oddly wooden and terribly sore. He tried to recollect who he was and where he was, but the knowledge eluded him. Then something softly stroked his forehead and from impossibly far away came a tender voice. He couldn't pinpoint the source, try as he might. Again something caressed his brow. A conviction came over him that he wasn't truly awake, that everything around him was the product of a dream. And with the conviction came consciousness.

"Husband! Oh, husband!"

Nate King felt warm hands on his neck and hot tears on his cheeks. "Winona?" he croaked. "Is that you?" A vision of loveliness floated above him, her face glistening. Her soft lips lovingly brushed his.

"Who else would make such a fuss over you?" Winona said, forcing a grin. She burst into more tears. "I was never so scared of losing you." Lowering her cheek to his chest, she enfolded him in her arms.

Small fingers entwined with Nate's own. A smaller version of his wife planted a kiss on his temple.

"You had us both powerful worried, Pa. If it hadn't been for those Utes, we'd have lost you. Zach still isn't back with the healer he went after."

"Utes?" Nate tried to sit up, but his arms weighed tons.

"Just lie there," Winona directed. "It will be days before you are strong enough to get out of bed." She paused. "An Ute named Neota came here looking for you. He showed us how to break your fever. Yesterday he had to leave. I promised him, on your behalf, that when you are fit enough you will repay his kindness."

"This Neota needs my help?"

"His whole tribe does. Eleven of their people have been killed by a grizzly. They say it hunts them for food, that it raids their villages and carries people off. Their warriors tried to slay it, but their arrows and lances have no effect.

158

So they held a council and decided to send Neota to appeal to the one man who might be able to help them." Winona beamed with pride. "The famous Grizzly Killer."

Nate's mouth went dry. Horrid images of the black bear tearing and rending at his body caused him to ball his fists until his nails bit into his palms.

"This will give you something to look forward to, Pa," Evelyn declared. "You used to say there aren't many grizzlies left to hunt in our neck of the woods. Now you get to go after one just like in the old days."

"Lucky me."

"Niwot told me you're their last hope. His people are counting on you."

"Niwot?"

"A young warrior," Winona answered in a tone that implied she wasn't excessively fond of him. "I will tell you about him later." She drew the blanket up to his chin. "Would you care for a bite to eat? I've been forcing soup down your throat, but you must be half starved."

At the mention of food, Nate's stomach rumbled.

Rising, Winona moved toward the counter. "You rest, husband, and leave everything to me. I will have you back on your feet before you know it."

Nate glanced at the bandage on his right shoulder and relived that awful moment when the black bear's teeth ripped his flesh open to the bone. "There's no hurry," he said. "No hurry at all."

Twilight was giving way to night when Zach King forded Dead Elk Creek and approached the trading post. He had taken off his buckskin shirt and replaced it with a homespun shirt from his saddlebags. Lou had crafted it from dark blue material, and it blended well into the gathering darkness. To further disguise his appearance he had folded a red handkerchief and tied it around his head. Now, adopting a friendly smile, he waved and shouted to the sentry. "Say

David Thompson

there! Are you coons open for business, or should I come back tomorrow?"

The sentry was fiddling with a folding knife. Giving a start, he snatched his rifle and bent over the rail. "Tarnation, mister! You about scared ten years' growth out of me! I didn't see you come riding up."

"Sorry, friend," Zach said, playing his part. "I didn't mean to spook you. This beaver feels a mite like chawing, is all."

"Got anything to trade?" the sentry asked.

"No," Zach admitted, then shook his possibles bag so the loose bullets he had dropped inside earlier rattled and clattered somewhat like money would. "But I've got me some coins to spend on hard liquor if there's any to be had."

"You've come to the right place. We've got some of the best drinking whiskey this side of the Mississippi." Pivoting, the sentry called down into the compound. "Harve! Get your carcass over here! There's a feller at the gate. Let him in."

Zach nodded amiably at the rough-hewn character who admitted him. The shout had drawn several whites from the trading post, and among them was one who answered to Touch the Clouds's description of Artemis Borke.

"Hold up there, hoss. Who might you be?"

"Scott Kendall," Zach fibbed. "I have a homestead a couple of days' ride from here. I was passing through and happened to spot your place, so I moseyed over for a look-see." Smacking his lips, he patted his possibles bag. "If you're willing, I'd like to treat myself to some rotgut. It's been ages since I had good sipping whiskey."

"You talk like a white man, but you sure don't look like one," Borke commented.

"I'm part Arapaho on my mother's side." Zach piled lie on top of lie. "My pa and her met back in the trapping days."

"I hear tell a lot of those old boys took up with squaws," Borke said. For a span of ten to fifteen seconds he gnawed

160

on his lower lip and then appeared to come to a decision. "Make yourself welcome. You can keep your horse in the stable overnight and bed down in the hay if you're of a mind to."

Zach dismounted. The Crow was taking his measure, but near as he could tell the warrior didn't recognize him. From the long building came rowdy mirth. Above the door hung a sign that read, "Snake River Trading Emporium." He noticed that there were no windows. "Wait until my friends hear about this place. You'll have customers lined up waiting to get in."

"The more the merrier," Borke said.

Zach heard the creak of leather hinges. A pair of whites were swinging the gate shut. He had hoped they would leave it open. Now the task he had set for himself would be doubly difficult. Which suited him just fine. He relished the impending combat. Relished the thought of counting coup. Relished the thrill of pitting his wits and brawn against an adversary as devious as Artemis Borke.

"We've got some Crows payin' a visit right this moment," Borke said, eyeing Zach speculatively to gauge his reaction.

"Just so they aren't Blackfeet," Zach responded. "I don't know about you, but I'm right partial to my hair."

Borke laughed. "I like you, sonny. You have a sense of humor. Come on in and I'll pour your first drink myself."

"Just so you're not stingy with the liquor." Zach allowed the older man to usher him through the doorway.

Lanterns lit the room as brightly as day. At the counter were five Crows, bottles in hand. Three more were hunkered over in a corner, one of them the warrior Zach had wounded. To a man, they glanced around sharply at his entrance.

Hoping his change of attire was enough to fool them, Zach smiled and brazenly strolled to an unoccupied table. A skinny white man was behind the bar; two others were at a far table playing cards. Conscious of being the focus of

David Thompson

attention, Zach eased into a chair and placed his rifle in front of him. He was trying to act casual, but a million butterflies were fluttering in his gut. All hell would break loose if any of the Crows recognized him. He doubted they got a good look at him, but he could be wrong.

Artemis Borke brought over a bottle of whiskey and two glasses and sank down across from him. "So tell me, Mr. Kendall. You've lived in these parts all your life, I take it?"

"Since I was knee-high to a cricket," Zach said.

"Then I bet you've heard tales of gold and silver being found from time to time. Like that mountaineer a few years ago who showed up in St. Louis with a poke full of nuggets as big as walnuts."

"Everyone hears stories," Zach said, and flicked a finger at the Crows, one of whom was guzzling whiskey as if it were water. "There's a rumor their tribe knows where to find some gold, but the Crows say it's not true."

"How about you? Do you know where to find some?"

About to reach for the drink Borke had poured, Zach was struck by the intense, almost feral expression of raw and total greed Borke bestowed on him. Then and there he knew why the trader had established the post. And why Borke was courting the Crows.

"If you did, I'd make it well worth your while to show me."

Zach savored a slow sip before replying. "I've never found any gold myself." Which was another lie. His father had shown him a stream high in the mountains where nuggets were as common as clover in a field. But they had no interest in gathering it up and moving back to civilization to live in opulent ease. They were content with their lives as they were. "I have a friend, though, who claims to know of a cave where there's so much gold, it practically blinds a body to look at it."

Borke rimmed his lips with the tip of his tongue like a starving man about to bite into a juicy steak. "You don't

162

say? Do you suppose I could impose on you to introduce me?"

"I suppose." Zach did not want to appear too eager or it would seem strange. He raised his glass again, and as he tilted his head back he noticed one of the Crows by the bar giving him an intent scrutiny. "But I wouldn't get your hopes up. He doesn't cotton to strangers much."

"You never know," Borke said with a shrug. "I can be pretty persuasive when I need to be."

The Crow whispered to another and the second warrior turned to stare. Zach took that as an omen. He needed an excuse to leave without arousing suspicion. "I reckon I'll take you up on your offer to use your stable tonight," he casually mentioned. "So maybe I should go tend to my horse before I drink so much I'm liable to forget."

"It can wait," Borke said. "Tell me more about this friend of yours."

"All I know is that it's way back in the high country, up above the snow line. It takes about a week to get there." The two Crows had nudged a third, and all three were studying him as if he were the first half-breed they ever met. Taking another sip, Zach placed the glass down and rose. "I really should bed down my animal. We've been on the trail since before first light."

"Suit yourself. I'll be waitin' right here."

Nodding, Zach ambled toward the door. He didn't like turning his back to the Crows, but it had to be done. His scalp itching as if from prickly heat, he passed a white man who had just entered and reached for the latch.

A fierce shriek rent the room. Not a heartbeat later, a knife flashed past Zach's cheek and embedded itself in the door with a loud *thunk*. He didn't glance behind him. He didn't stop. Yanking on the latch, he sprang out into the night with another shriek ringing in his ears. Shouts erupted, Artemis Borke bellowing loudest of all.

Another of the trader's accomplices was a few yards

away, sharpening a knife. He glanced at the doorway, then at Zach, and lunged, his blade raised to slash.

Ducking under the blow, Zach twisted and slammed the Hawken's stock against the man's forehead. It felled him like a heart-shot elk. Instantly, Zach ran on, but not toward the dun. He had to accomplish what he had set out to do or his life would be forfeit. Necessity lending wings to his feet, he sprinted toward the gate.

"You there! Stop or I'll shoot!"

The sentry was raising his rifle. Without breaking stride Zach did likewise, his Hawken cracking a split second before the sentry's rifle boomed. A slug whistled past his left ear. Up on the tower the sentry grabbed at his chest, tottered backward, and disappeared over the far rail.

Zach chanced a look back. Crows and whites were spilling from the trading post in a savage jumble. The warrior watching the warhorses had recovered from his initial confusion and was drawing back the sinew string to his bow. Zach veered just as the shaft shot toward him. It missed, but not by more than a cat's whisker.

Forty feet more and Zach would be there. But the gate might as well be in Missouri. Gunfire rocked the night as leaden hornets sought his blood. Another arrow streaked out of the gloom and he felt a twinge of pain in his right arm. The barbed tip had sliced through his shirt, creasing him.

"Stop that bastard!" Artemis Borke raged. "He's the one the Crows tangled with this afternoon!"

The warriors were bounding in pursuit, yipping and howling at the top of their lungs, out to repay Zach for getting the better of them.

A rifle cracked and a ball buzzed within an inch of Zach's neck. A bow string twanged and a glittering shaft nearly clipped his ear. Only the enveloping darkness saved him. The traders hadn't gotten around to lighting any outside lanterns yet and the compound was mired in murk.

Zach flew the final ten feet, dropped his Hawken, and gripped the long wooden bar that secured the gate. Another arrow thudded into the wood near his elbow. A slug ripped into the gate above his head.

"Stop him!" Artemis Borke screamed.

Feet smacked the earth to Zach's rear. Letting go of the bar, he whirled, his right hand swooping to one of the pistols at his waist. An onrushing Crow with an upraised war club was almost on top of him. Snapping back the hammer, Zach fired when the Crow was only two strides away. His aim was true. The shot took the Crow low on the jaw and exploded out the rear of his cranium, killing him, but the warrior's momentum carried him forward the final few feet and he would have slammed into Zach with the impact of a charging buffalo if Zach hadn't leaped aside.

More Crows were streaming toward him in a frenzy of bloodlust.

Spinning, Zach locked his arms on the bar and slid it up over the braces. He tossed it down, pushed on the gate, and attempted to turn to confront his attackers. But a glancing blow to the side of his head buckled him to his knees. The world swam and danced. Shaking his head to clear it, he looked up into the hate-filled eyes of a brawny Crow about to dash out his brains.

The Crow sneered in triumph. And the next moment he was dead on his feet, the feathered end of a Shoshone arrow jutting from his ribs.

Shoshone war cries rose above the din as through the open gate hurtled Touch the Clouds and Drags the Rope at the head of the war party. Three stunned Crows were caught flat-footed. With ruthless efficiency, the Shoshones slashed through them like scythes through grain. More guns thundered. The whites and the remaining Crows retreated toward the trading post, Borke yelling commands no one could hear.

Zach heaved upright, drawing his other pistol. Steadying

himself, he took a deliberate bead at Borke's face, but a skinny white blundered between them just as he fired. Borke backpedaled into the trading post followed by other underlings, and slammed the door. The next moment a long, slender object slid through a loophole in the front wall.

"Take cover!" Zach shouted in Shoshone, but it was too late. The rifle spat lead and smoke and a Shoshone dropped.

Casting about for his other guns, Zach scooped them up and moved into inky blackness to reload. As he opened his powder horn another rifle was thrust through a loophole, but the hasty shot missed.

Touch the Clouds was urging his warriors to seek shelter. Few heeded him. They had lost too many friends and wouldn't rest until they had repaid those responsible. Screeching like banshees, they threw themselves at the door, seeking to bust it down.

Zach's fingers moved with practiced skill. He had reloaded his guns so many times, he could do it with his eyes shut if he had to. The routine never varied: pour in the powder, wedge a ball and patch into the muzzle, tamp both down with a ramrod. In no time he had his rifle and spent pistols reloaded and was racing to join the fray.

The Shoshones had found a log somewhere and were battering at the door like medieval knights at a castle. A crack had appeared in the center and was widening swiftly, infusing the Shoshones with renewed vigor. A pistol barked and one of their number fell, only to be immediately replaced by another. A Crow arrow transfixed a Shoshone's arm, but the warrior hardly slowed.

Zach weaved around fallen Crows, eager to get there before the Shoshones broke inside. He leaped over the skinny white he had slain and was in among the warriors at the door, yipping with the best of them. At their next swing of the log the door crumpled like so much paper. Inside, four or five guns blasted and several Shoshones fell. The rest wavered.

Zach darted past into the mushrooming clouds of gun smoke. He figured the whites needed time to reload, but one materialized in front of him, armed with a pistol. Zach shoved the Hawken's muzzle against the man's stomach and fired. Letting the rifle follow the white to the floor, he whipped out both pistols and shot a Crow on his left and another white man on his right. Another gun discharged over by the counter, but the bullet came nowhere near him.

Discarding his spent pistols, Zach unlimbered his butcher knife and tomahawk and waded deeper into the smoke. Suddenly there were whites and Crows on all sides. Knives and war clubs and lances sought his heart and jugular. Zach responded in kind, swinging and stabbing and hacking and dodging. He felt the tomahawk bite into bone, felt his knife shear into flesh. Curses and screams pummeled his ears. He slashed. He cut. He ducked under a war club and sank his tomahawk into the wielder.

Then the smoke parted and there, not a yard away, stood Artemis Borke. Borke had just reloaded a pistol, and at the sight of Zach he jerked it up to fire. It was not quite level when Zach's tomahawk cleaved Borke's skull like a soggy melon, clean down to the top of the trader's nose.

A deafening silence gripped the room. Zach glanced about for new foes, every nerve on fire. But there were none. Bodies lay on all sides, two deep in spots. He was caked with sweat, blood, and gore, and breathing as if he had run ten miles. Sucking in a breath, he slowly turned, grateful for a gust of cool air.

Touch the Clouds and Drags the Rope stood just inside. Other Shoshones filled the doorway or gazed over the shoulders of those in front. To a man, their faces betrayed shock. Shock and something else, something akin to awe.

"What?"

Touch the Clouds surveyed the slaughter and said softly, "Truly, you are the son of Grizzly Killer."

Stepping over grotesquely contorted shapes, Zach moved

toward the door. As he stepped into the open, he acquired a shadow twice his size.

"Stalking Coyote, we must have words."

"I know what you are about to say," Zach responded, "and you can stop worrying. The whites will not declare war on the Shoshones."

"How can you be certain?" Touch the Clouds asked. "We have killed their own kind."

"I killed the whites," Zach amended. "But I won't be blamed, either."

"Then who will?" Touch the Clouds was genuinely confused.

Zach walked to a slain Crow and nudged the body with a toe. "Three guesses. I told you I would take care of everything. Only white and Crow remains will be found in the ashes."

"Ashes?"

"After I burn the place down." Zach grinned. "Word will reach Bent's Fort that the Crows attacked the post and in a pitched battled wiped them out. During the fight a lantern was knocked over and it set the buildings on fire. If other whites come to investigate, all they will find are charred embers and a few Crow arrowheads and arrows I will leave lying about."

Touch the Clouds's face was inscrutable. "You would do such a thing?"

"I will do whatever it takes to spare the Shoshones harm." Zach straightened. "Trust me. The whites will never learn the truth. Everything will work out fine."

Afterword

Zachary King was wrong. But that is a tale for another time.

Historians of the fur trade have long wondered about conflicting accounts of a trading post on the Green River. Bridger and Smith said there was one; Walker and Meek make no mention of it. At last we know the truth. Once again the private journals of Nate King have come in handy.

No one disputes King's long struggle against the most vicious killer grizzly in the history of North America. In a sense this book is a prelude to the story of Scar, as the bear became known. It is a riveting clash of man versus beast the likes of which we have seldom seen. Before it was over, more than forty Utes and other victims were dead. Yes, you read correctly. Over forty. In the annals of animal attacks, the havoc Scar wreaked almost rivals the carnage caused by the fabled Beast of Gevaudan.

And that is our tale for next time.